THAWING THE VISCOUNT'S HEART

BELLES OF CHRISTMAS:FROST FAIR

MINDY BURBIDGE STRUNK

Cover Art by Ashtyn Newbold

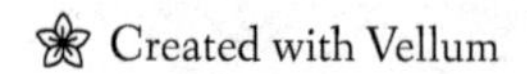

CHAPTER 1

Gabrielle Babineaux shivered. She pulled her pelisse tighter around her middle. Her bonnet pulled taut against the ribbons tied beneath her chin as she stepped down from the carriage and looked down Thames Street. There was scarcely an empty space, so many carriages lined the street. It seemed everyone in London was intent on visiting the Grand Mall—the small patch of the Thames between the Blackfriars and London Bridges.

Gabby stepped to the railing and looked over the ground which normally separated the roadway from the now frozen river below. Tradesman carts and tents lined both sides of the actual river, while the middle was crowded with people standing shoulder to shoulder. Gabby shivered again, not from the cold, but rather from the thought of what so much weight on the ice could cause.

Chills ran down her spine, whether from her thoughts or the cold, she was not certain. Never could she remember feeling so cold in all her life. It wasn't a long one, but she'd been around enough to have some experience. And in that experience, she'd found England's people to be nearly as cold as her weather.

"It is called the *City Road.*" Lady Kirtley stepped up beside

Gabby and peered down at the ice. "It seems we are not the only ones to venture out to the fair today." She glanced at the line of carriages and then back to the *City Road*. "Perhaps it won't be so bad with all these people about. They will surely help to block the winds." Lady Kirtley buried her hands further in her muff. "It is unbearably cold today." She sighed and a puff of air showed in front of her face. "But then, I suppose without this cold, we could not have the fair, now, could we?"

Lord Kirtley pulled his wife to his side. "We will be warmer if we stay close together, I think." He grinned down at her and Gabby looked away, her face warming.

"Did you not say Peter was coming?" Gabrielle asked, her French accent becoming thicker as the cold seeped deep into her bones.

While she enjoyed Lady Kirtley's company and was grateful for her sponsorship for the upcoming Season, it was Peter she felt more comfortable with. Peter— or rather, Lord Rockwell when they were in public—was like a brother to her.

"He and Caroline should be here shortly. But we do not need them for entertainment." Lady Kirtley put her hand at the small of Gabrielle's back and gave her a slight push forward. "Come, let us see what we can find. I can smell the roasted mutton from here."

They ventured down Three Crane Stairs to the riverfront. Lord Kirtley had thought the crowds would be less at Queen Street, Cheapside, but he had been wrong. There was no place that was not swarming with people.

"Is this...fair a common occurrence?" Gabby placed one foot onto the ice, tentatively testing her weight. This all felt so unnatural.

Her grandfather had told her stories of the days when the Rhone had frozen over, and men could walk from one side to the other. But that had been nearly one hundred and fifty years ago. In truth, Gabby had always supposed the tale to be just that—a story. She didn't think her grandfather dishonest, but rather the story had grown as the years went on.

Lady Kirtley shook her head. "Yes, well, common enough."

Gabby glanced over her shoulder at Lady Kirtley. "Then you have seen it before. This is what I am to expect of England?" There had been some snow last year, but it had not been so cold as it was now.

"Well, not exactly. I was only five at the last fair, but I've heard tales about it happening for years. The conditions have not been just so until recently." Lady Kirtley pointed to the center of the ice. "Look, there are already many people out on the ice, and it is holding perfectly well. I am certain we shall be safe."

Was that hesitation in her voice?

Gabby eyed the lady, her credibility losing some of its hold.

"Come, Miss Babineaux. This is just the event for us to begin your introductions into society." She glanced around them. "Much of the *Ton* are still at their country estates. But there are a fair number that remain in London. It shall not be so overwhelming now and will hopefully allow you to know some young ladies once the Season begins in earnest."

Gabby had thought the notion of a Season exciting when Lady Kirtley and Peter had discussed it upon Gabrielle's arrival several years ago. But now that the time approached, her confidence waned.

Her accent was still thicker than she wanted it to be, something that Lady Kirtley likewise feared would hinder her success in the coming Season. She still slipped into her native tongue when she was nervous or emotional—or apparently cold. She'd heard what could happen if the *Ton* did not believe a person worthy of their attentions. She was not looking forward to discovering exactly what they *thought* of her.

She bit down on the inside of her cheek. The more she focused on it, the more she thought staying at Dovehaven a much better idea. Surely there were ladies who had found a match without participating in a Season. Could she not try her luck that way? Perhaps God would look favorably on her and she would happen upon the gentleman while taking a walk into Appledore. After all, Kent was a desirable county with plenty of eligible gentlemen.

Perhaps she would mention it to Lady Kirtley...Gabby cringed. Or perhaps not.

Gabby took light steps on the ice, still not convinced that this endeavor was entirely safe. Hoots and shouting came from somewhere amid the tents. A young boy, his friends cheering him on, kicked a leather ball to a gentleman.

Gabby smiled at the tenderness of the scene. She did not know many gentlemen who would take the time to play ball with a child.

The ball went wide, and the gentleman raced after it, but before he could stop it, his foot shot out from beneath him.

Instinctively, Gabby reached out to the side, in search of something to steady her, though she found nothing there. Her mouth dropped open as a young lady stepped directly into the gentleman's slippery path. Within mere seconds, the two were nothing but a heap on the ice.

Looking down at the ice in front of her, Gabby again questioned the prudence of this excursion.

Lady Kirtley glanced at the ruckus but guided Gabby in the opposite direction. A tent directly in front of them swelled with people, smoke billowing out a hole in the top. The smell of roasting meat permeated the air. "Come, Miss Babineaux, let us go and see what is happening in there. Perhaps we can even purchase some of the *Lapland Mutton*. I've heard it is delicious. Indeed, I have very faint memories of it from when I was a child."

They approached the tent door and Lord Kirtley paid a sixpence each for them to enter. A fire burned in a large iron pan, the lamb suspended just high enough that it did not touch the wood, now mostly burned down to coals.

The man behind the fire carved off sections of the charred meat and offered it to anyone able and willing to pay the price.

"It smells wonderful, does it not?" A gentleman stood next to Gabrielle. He ran his tongue over his lips, his eyes widening as the flames licked up the sides of the lamb. "Are you to buy a slice?"

Gabby shook her head. "I should zink not."

"You're French," the man said.

She did not have to turn to look at his face to know of his opinion of her. She had never heard so much disdain and outright anger in two words.

Gabby took a step closer to Lady Kirtley whose attention was on the mutton.

Gabby flicked her gaze to the man. "*Oui*—yes. But I live in Kent now."

The man's nose curled, and he turned away pushing his way through the crowd and out the tent flap.

"Would you like some meat, Miss Babineaux?" Lady Kirtley only now turned her attention to Gabby.

Gabby shook her head, her stomach clenching, and her hands shaking. The once enticing smell now brought her morning tea and ham too close to the surface. "It is far too crowded in here. I zink I shall step outside for a breath of air." She turned and pushed her way to the tent entrance, pausing a moment, hoping the *gentleman* had put a fair amount of distance between himself and the tent. The last thing she wanted was to see him again.

She closed her eyes and pushed aside the flap, breathing in deeply as she cleared the tent walls. Icy shards filled her lungs, her chest instantly aching. Still, it was preferable to the confines inside.

You're French. She wrapped her arms around her middle, the voice echoing inside her mind. Such treatment should not bother her any longer. *He* was not the first to behave in such a way. It was more common than not, which was one of the reasons Lady Kirtley felt it important for Gabby to sound as English as possible before the Season began.

Gabby took in a stuttering breath.

Lady Kirtley's request was easier said than done. Gabby just could not seem to make her tongue form the English sounds no matter how hard she tried.

She stood next to the tent entrance, waiting for Lord and Lady Kirtley to receive their meat and come fetch her.

Cold seeped up through the soles of her half-boots; her toes and feet felt as if hundreds of little pins poked into her skin. She stomped the ground several times, hoping to infuse some warmth into her body, but then remembered she was standing on ice. How much of it separated her from the frigid water below she did not know. Best to keep her movements as smooth and light as possible.

"A memento of the *Great Frost,* miss?" A boy came forward, shoving a sheet of paper under her nose. Gabby read the advertisement.

Behold the River Thames is frozen o'er,
Which, lately ships of mighty burden bore;
Now, different arts and pastimes here you see,
But printing claims superiority.

Gabby was about to hand the paper back when she looked at the boy and his shabby clothes. She opened her reticule and took out a coin, placing it in his outstretched hand. It would make a nice souvenir, and if it helped put food in this small boy's belly, even better.

The boy hurried off to his next customer, hollering over his shoulder. "Thank ye, miss."

Gabby smiled at him and tucked the paper in her reticule before pulling the strings tight. She looked up and let out a little squeal. Finally, *he* was here.

She looked back at the tent entrance, but no one came out. Shrugging, she moved quicker than Lady Kirtley would surely find proper toward the couple walking on the other side of the *City Road.* "Lady Rockwell." Gabby lifted a hand.

"Miss Babineaux," Lady Kirtley hollered behind her.

Gabby turned her head back, but her momentum carried her forward several steps where she collided with something solid. Stumbling backward, she wondered how a bridge support could have come out of nowhere. It was only when strong hands reached out to steady her that Gabby realized her mistake. This was no bridge support.

"Forgive me, miss. I must not have been paying attention. Are you well?" His voice was deep and had the slightest hint of gravel to it. Gabby shivered, having never been so affected by the mere sound of a voice.

She looked up into his smiling face. "*Excusez-moi*...er, please excuse me, sir." Gabby put a hand to his chest, his slate-blue eyes drawing her in. But both their smiles dropped away.

It was *him*. The man from the tent who had been so unabashedly rude upon learning she was French.

He dropped his hands from her arms and took several steps back, his eyes narrowing. "Oh. It is *you*," he said. He cleared his throat and straightened his coat. "You did not answer my question. Are you well?" Though his words said one thing, his tone said completely another.

Gabby swallowed and pulled her gaze from his stony face. How could a man *si beau* be so very unpleasant?

She ran her hands down the front of her dress. "Yes. I am well, zanks to your swift actions, sir."

He gave her a curt nod. "Then I will beg your forgiveness and bid you farewell." His left eye twitched slightly as he turned on his heel, and quickly strode into the crowd.

Lord and Lady Rockwell walked swiftly from one direction as Lord and Lady Kirtley came from the other, all forming a tight circle around her.

"Are you harmed, Gabby?" Lady Rockwell put a hand on Gabby's arm, her face etched with concern. While the lady was firm in her training, Gabby had no doubt that Lady Kirtley cared about her.

Gabby shook her head as she rubbed at her hip.

"Gabrielle."

Gabby knew the level of concern Lady Kirtley must feel if she was resorting to using her Christian name while they were in public.

"What were you thinking, paying so little heed to where you were going?" Lady Kirtley's hand patted Gabby's back, lessening the sting of her harsh words.

"I am well. You need not worry." She craned her neck, hoping to catch another glimpse of the gentleman. She did not know why she wished to see his scrunched-up nose and curled lips. Perhaps it was because she now knew what he could look like when he smiled, and that was truly something to behold. She knew he would never again share such a smile with her. But one more glimpse wouldn't hurt.

"I am glad you were not injured. Mr. Campbell is not a slight man. I imagine he could do you some serious injury." Lord Kirtley gave her a fatherly pat on the shoulder.

Gabby placed gloved hands to her heated cheeks. "As you can see, Mr. Campbell ensured I did not sustain injury, so we can continue our outing."

"You are certain?" Peter raised a brow.

Gabby nodded, wishing their scrutiny would come to an end.

Peter sighed and looked off into the crowd. "I wish he'd not hurried off so quickly. I should like to have talked to him before he returns to the continent."

"The continent? Why would he be going sere?" Gabby wrapped her pelisse tighter.

Peter held one arm out to her and one to his wife. "He is in the army. A major, if I remember correctly. I can only assume he is on leave for the holidays."

Gabby looked back toward the crowd. The man was in the army, fighting against Napoleon. She raised a brow. Perhaps that was the reason for his less than polite behavior? Although, why he should blame Napoleon and his actions on her, she did not understand.

CHAPTER 2

Aaron Campbell walked away from the crowds gathered on the River Thames, his fists clenching at his side and his heart hammering in his chest. He climbed the Old Swell stairs, his breath coming easier the more distance he put between himself and that French antagonist from the mutton tent.

Her innocent act did not fool him. He'd fallen for that French trick once before and he would never do it again. Mireille's face floated into his mind and he squeezed his fingers tighter. His shoulders tightened as her voice replayed in his mind. *Zank you, Major.* While the woman from the tent did not look much like Mireille—she was much younger and much pret—

No. Aaron pushed the thought away with an angry sigh.

Would there ever come a time when he didn't flinch at the sound of that accent?

He rotated his shoulders as he climbed into the Brinton carriage, rapping on the side as he settled back against the seat. The barouche jerked forward, moving slowly until they cleared Thames Street. Aaron dropped his head back and closed his eyes. Even with the crowds behind them, the icy streets were bound to make it a long drive home.

He had been having an enjoyable time at the fair, an unexpected diversion from his new responsibilities. But then he'd encountered *her*. Her, with her small button nose and caramel-colored eyes. He growled, irritated that he'd even noticed her eyes. Why, amidst all those people, did he have to encounter the one French woman who sounded so...*French*?

He stared out the window, watching as Grace Church Street and Cheapside passed by. People milled about as if everything was normal. Did they not remember a war with a madman raged on the Continent?

Aaron's hands were damp inside his gloves, making them feel colder than they should. His heart thumped harder in his chest. "I should be there." He pounded his fist on the velvet-covered bench, his stomach burning. He should be with his men, fighting alongside them, not at his family's London Townhome where one was never in want of warmth or food. This life he was living was ridiculous.

His hand went to his cravat. Had not Martin spent the better part of half an hour tying this blasted knot? It was a knot of his valet's own imagination. Something about a mathematical with a twist? He fingered the noose at his throat. Out of principle, he should yank it out and tie a simple waterfall, instead.

Aaron released a great sigh and dropped his head back, looking up at the ceiling. But what would that prove? It is not as if his men would know of his act of unity.

The carriage pulled to a stop in front of Larkspur House. Aaron looked up at the beige stonework. It was ridiculous to have a house in town when the family estate was only a day's ride from London—albeit a very long day. But this house had been in the family for nearly a hundred years and trying to convince his mother to let it go—she'd likely only yield if it was to move them to the more fashionable Grosvenor Square—was a discussion he just didn't have in him.

The carriage door opened, and Aaron stepped out onto the walk.

The wind blew down the street, picking up his greatcoat and pulling it away from his body. He quickly reached a hand up to keep his beaver in place.

He glanced back up at the windows dotting the front of the house. He had thought to stay in Town for a few days longer, but anxiety was pushing him to leave for Ivydale Hall immediately. He would just need to convince his mother to leave early.

He mounted the stairs to their Hanover Square house and nodded to the footman at the door. He should remember the man's name, but he didn't. It seemed his brother had replaced more than half the staff since Father had died four years earlier. Maybe that was why he preferred Ivydale. Here, he felt like a stranger in his own home.

"Back so soon, dearest?" His mother looked up from the floral arrangement she fussed with in the entry hall.

"The crowds were greater than I anticipated. It is hard for one to enjoy the festivities when you cannot take a step without bumping into someone." The French girl's face came to his mind, and he growled low in his throat. Would her image occupy his mind for the remainder of the day? What if it stayed there longer?

He handed off his greatcoat and hat to Collins. At least the family butler was still here. Aaron was grateful for that small bit of continuity.

"You should have expected as much. The fair is popular with both society and the lower classes. I'm sure Henry would have found pleasure in such a gathering." His mother pulled out a large flower and moved it to a different location within the vase.

A knot lodged in Aaron's throat. *Henry.*

Henry was why Aaron was home. If Aaron had stayed in France, as he wished, his mother would be here, dealing with the untimely death of Henry alone. It seemed an impossible situation. Whichever path he chose, he would inevitably feel guilt for abandoning someone.

His brother's death had not been part of Aaron's long-term plan.

Henry was to be the Viscount—Lord Brinton—and pass the title on to his children. Their father had trained Henry to assume the title, while Aaron was left to make his mark in the military. But now that was all changed.

When word of Henry's death had reached Aaron, it was expected that he would sell his commission and come home immediately to assume the title that should never have been his. There was also the matter of his mother and brother's widow's care.

He scrubbed his hand back and forth through his hair. At least Rebekah had remained back at Ivydale.

"Yes, well, Henry always was an amiable gentleman." He took the stairs two at a time, unable to reach the study quick enough. He paused at the first-floor landing and turned back. "Mother, I have decided we are to travel to Ivydale Hall earlier than planned. Please prepare to leave first thing on the morrow. I should not like to spend a night at an inn, so our departure will be an early one."

He turned and hurried down the corridor before his mother could begin her arguments against it; he knew her well enough to know they would be coming.

He pushed into the study and closed the door behind him, grateful for the dimly lit room. It was quiet and made him feel sheltered, even if he felt like he was invading a space that was never intended to be his.

Aaron grabbed the ledgers off the desk and moved over to the settee next to the fire. He stretched out, opening the first book on his lap. This was not the most ideal place to look over the books but sitting behind the desk still felt odd. Aaron had seen his father behind the desk all of his life. He did not know if he would ever feel comfortable behind it.

A knock sounded on the door, and he grunted. His mother had come quicker than he'd expected. Although, it shouldn't have surprised him. She was still a spry woman at the age of five and fifty.

"Come in."

As he suspected, his mother entered and sat in the chair across from him. "Why are we returning to the country early? I have already accepted several invitations for the next few nights. It will be most inconvenient to cancel them at this late date."

Aaron sighed and crossed one leg over the other, gripping his knee with clasped hands. "It is colder than usual, mother. I fear if we hold off, there will be a storm and we may not make it to Ivydale for the holidays."

"Staying in town for Christmastide would not be so very terrible." His mother's lips pursed tightly in a line.

Aaron breathed in patience. "Perhaps. But it would leave Lady Brinton alone and in her current situation, I think that unkind. I'm sure people would understand you declining the invitations. After all, you are well respected among the *Ton*."

She sighed, narrowing her eyes at him. "And how do you think I earned that respect? It was not by canceling engagements at the last minute." She clasped her hands in her lap, a sure sign of irritation. "When did you become an expert on the weather anyhow? If Henry were here, I'm sure he would let us wait at least until after Lord Trenton's annual ball."

Aaron twisted his head slightly to the side and stared at the burgundy spine of the book just over his mother's shoulder. *If Henry were here.* The phrase had become commonplace in his mother's vocabulary. Aaron was fast becoming sick of it. He mourned Henry but was finding it increasingly difficult to live up to his brother's memory. Henry had become a giant among men *since* his death.

Aaron released his knee, cringing inwardly at the unkind thought. He looked heavenward. My *apologies, Henry.*

"Yes, well, unfortunately, Henry is not here, Mother. I am. And I have decided we leave tomorrow. You may bring your trunks along or you may leave them here. Regardless of what you choose, you will be in the carriage before dawn."

She huffed, narrowing her eyes at him for the second time in as many minutes. "I am not one of your soldiers to order about as you wish. I am your mother and the Dowager Viscountess Brinton. You will show me the respect I deserve."

Aaron's knuckles whitened as he gripped the arms of his seat. "Please, Mother, will you be ready to depart at dawn?" He spoke through gritted teeth.

She sniffed. "I cannot say for certain yet. I have letters to write before I can let you know one way or the other."

Aaron clenched his jaw tightly to keep from barking out a response he knew he would regret later. "How about a compromise?" He leaned forward, resting his elbows on his knees. "I am leaving on the morrow. If you wish to join me, I shall see you in the carriage before first light. If not, I will try to send it back to retrieve you, as long as the weather permits."

"That is no compromise." His mother shot to her feet and glared down at him. "You would leave me behind to make my way to Ivydale unprotected? If Henry were here—"

Aaron raised his hand. "Yes, yes. I know. He would never allow you to travel alone." His interruption only served to increase her glare and the flare of her nostrils. It really was a most unbecoming sight, but he would not touch on that point now.

He matched her stare. Would it be too much to hope that she would avoid Ivydale altogether for the Christmastide?

He frowned. If his mother did not come, it would leave him alone with Lady Brinton for the holidays. Not that he disliked his brother's widow—he barely knew her—but the few days he'd spent at the family estate before coming to Town had been filled with lamenting and tears. Aaron did not deal well with watering pots. And a fortnight seemed an impossible amount of time to put up with one. At least on his own. "I would appreciate knowing your plans as soon as possible. I will need to let Cook know how much food to prepare for the hamper."

His mother's head shook in obvious disgust. "You are not even to allow us to leave the carriage to eat our meals? You really are a pinch pocket, Aaron."

Aaron rubbed at his eyes with his thumb and forefinger. It was not about the money as much as the time. If they stopped for food every time they switched out the horses, they would not make it to the estate until well after dark. His mother was not one for purchasing some cheese and bread to make do. She would require a full spread at each mealtime.

Lud, he was tired of this argument already. He grunted. "I may be persuaded to make some concessions, Mother." He looked toward the door. "But now I must write to Mrs. Hawkins and make her aware of our early return. If you'll excuse me."

She huffed at the dismissal but turned to leave. "I hope this demanding attitude of yours is only temporary. I do not relish living under a tyrant." She lifted her chin and toddled out of the room.

A smile twitched at Aaron's mouth. *Tyrant.* Well now, maybe that was a title he could get behind.

CHAPTER 3

Gabby watched as Phillip hefted the last trunk up into the carriage. A small snowflake fluttered down, resting on the sash bar. She watched until the breeze picked it up and dropped it to the ground below.

Looking out at the gray sky, she noticed the snowflake was not a solitary one. Several more blew around the window and down near the carriage. Aline folded a shawl and gently stuffed it into the satchel on the bed.

Her bedroom door opened, and Molly came in. "Are you nearly ready, miss?" She ran a hand over the pristine counterpane. "Lady Kirtley is already waiting in the entry."

Gabby looked around the room one last time. She didn't know why she was feeling so sentimental. She would be back in this room in just over a fortnight. Heaving a sigh, she fastened the few buttons on her pelisse and hurried from the room.

"I am sorry to have kept you waiting, my lady." She dipped a hasty curtsy once both feet were on the marble entry floor.

Lady Kirtley placed a hand on Gabby's arm. "We are not in public, Gabrielle. You are welcome to call me Eleanor."

Gabby smiled out of politeness. She had lived with the Kirtleys for years. In the beginning, she had felt a part, like she was one of the family. She'd played with the children and, indeed, was treated like one of the Kirtleys' own. But in the last year, Gabby had noticed a change. As Lady Kirtley prepared Gabby for her come out, Gabby felt less at ease around the lady.

Lady Kirtley was not unkind; she was just so...very proper. It was the kind of proper that Gabby knew she would never achieve which made her feel as though she would always be a disappointment to those supporting her. And that thought worried Gabby.

She twisted the tip of her kid glove. She would always speak with too much of an accent and didn't think she would ever fully understand the workings of the British Ton. It was, no doubt, similar to the *beau monde* in France, but she had meant little to that society also. Her father had made a good living, but it did not put them in the ranks of the upper class.

Lady Kirtley guided Gabby toward the front door, the footman opening it as they approached. Snow swirled in the air outside, much heavier than it had been only moments ago.

Gabby stopped. "Is it safe to travel in this weather?"

Lady Kirtley nodded. "Oh, this is nothing. I've been assured it is far too cold for much snow to fall. We will be well."

Two carriages sat in front of Penderton House. The children and governess were already in the second one, and Lord Kirtley stood at the first, ready to hand his wife up.

Lady Kirtley settled in and her husband climbed in beside her. Phillip stepped forward to help Gabby. It was times like this that she felt like an intruder and she missed her papa most keenly.

She nodded to the footman and ducked as she stepped inside, sitting on the seat opposite the Kirtleys. Her breath puffed out in front of her face, her nose already prickling with cold. Pulling a rug onto her lap, she put her feet on the hot bricks, relishing the warmth radiating up through the soles of her half-boots.

Lord and Lady Kirtley huddled close to each other, speaking in hushed tones.

Gabby turned toward the window, seeing nothing that passed by. Her shoulders slumped, a thickness forming in her throat. If only Peter and Caroline had come with them, maybe she would not feel so lonely. She didn't even know if they would come to Kent for Christmastide.

She rested her head against the window, loneliness settling over her like a thick, woolen cloak.

The day went on in monotony. Ride in silence, change horses and grab a bite of food, then back in the carriage only to repeat over and over, even after the sun had set. She did not feel sleepy, but boredom pulled her eyes closed as darkness settled in.

The carriage jerked hard to the left and Gabby cracked her eyes open. It then jerked to the right, slamming Gabby hard against the side, her face smashing up against the glass. She let out a yelp as her shoulder burned with pain. What was happening?

"Gabrielle, are you hurt?" Lady Kirtley's hand rested on her leg. "We've had an accident."

Gabby pushed herself upright, looking around the carriage now leaning sharply forward. "What has happened?"

"The weather has worsened. We were hoping to make it to the next village before stopping, but it appears we pushed our luck too far." Lord Kirtley threw the rug off his lap and stooped to look out the window. "I am guessing we have broken an axle. We will not be going any farther in this carriage. Let me see if Harry has any notion of where we are. Perhaps we can all fit into the other carriage with the children and make it far enough to find adequate shelter."

He pushed open the carriage door, wind and snow blowing in and swirling about. The door slammed shut with force and Lord Kirtley disappeared into the darkness.

Gabby blinked rapidly. The carriage was damaged? How would they all fit into the other carriage? Three children, the nurse, and the governess already made it quite full. They would be on top of each other if Gabby and the Kirtleys had to join them.

She sniffed, her nose nearly numb from the cold. But being a little crowded seemed better than freezing to death.

"Do not fear, Gabrielle. I'm certain Hugh has a plan." Lady Kirtley's tone held the same note of uncertainty as it had at the Frost Fair. Her words seemed as much for her own benefit as for Gabby's.

Gabby chewed on the side of her cheek, the cold seeping through her cloak and woolen dress. It settled in her bones. What would they do if they could not find shelter?

The door opened again and Lord Kirtley stuck his head in. "We are in luck. Ivydale Hall is within a league of here."

"Ivydale?" Lady Kirtley's face scrunched up. "I've heard of it, but I don't recall the resident's name." She grasped her husband's hand and ducked out of the carriage, her voice fading.

Gabby leaned forward, hoping to hear who lived at Ivydale; she wouldn't recognize the name, but still found herself curious to know.

Snow blew in tight circles around the inside of the carriage. Perhaps it did not matter who the owner of the estate was as long as they could get out of the cold. She ducked through the door, the wind blowing snow into her eyes like little ice daggers.

Phillip reached up and grasped hold of her arm, helping her step down onto the road. The snow already came up past the tops of her half-boots. Icy water ran down past her ankles, settling in the space between her foot and the lining of her boot.

She squinted to look back at the second carriage. Lord Kirtley was already handing Lady Kirtley inside.

"Come, Miss Babineaux. We need to get you into the other carriage. The weather is not improving any. We must be on our way." Phillip guided her over and handed her up.

The inside of the carriage was tight, to be sure. Miss Carter, the governess, held Katie on her lap. The girl's eyes looked tired and worried. Nurse Jones held Sophia on her lap. The not yet two-year-old let out a little snore as she snuggled into her nurse's bosom.

Lord and Lady Kirtley sat on the seat beside their son. He was still a slight boy, leaving them enough room on the bench to be comfortable. Gabby looked at the small space left.

Nurse Jones was a stout woman, taking up more space on the bench than Miss Carter. Unfortunately, Miss Carter was not a wisp of a creature either. Gabby sighed and squeezed into the slight space between the two women. She brought her shoulders up, nearly touching them to her ears, to keep them from rubbing the other women's arms. There was little she could do about their legs.

The carriage set off at a slow pace. Gabby was not sure if the driver was taking it easy so as not to crash this carriage also, or if the extra weight and building snow was taxing the four horses.

"Did you say you know the owner of the estate?" She looked to Lord Kirtley, biting the inside of her lip. It was not her place to ask questions, but she could not help it.

"Ivydale is just up the lane. It is the estate of Lord Brinton. He is the brother of a friend from my Eton days." Lord Kirtley smiled down at his wife as if she'd been the one to ask the question. "I'm confident he will take us in until the weather clears. He will also know of someone who can fix the axle on the other carriage."

"What is to happen to the other carriage?" Gabby could not remember which of the carriages held her trunk, not that she hoped anyone would have to be without their things.

"Phillip will stay with the carriage until we send this one back to fetch him and the trunks. Then once the weather clears, we will fetch the carriage for repair."

Gabby looked out at the worsening storm. Poor Phillip. Would he be completely frozen by the time the carriage returned for him? "Are you certain Lord Brinton is at home?" Gabby grimaced again at her forwardness. But she did not receive a look of reproach from Lady Kirtley, so perhaps she was not completely out of line. Either that or the lady wanted to know the answer as badly as Gabby.

"I did not see him in town, so perhaps he is staying at the estate until after Christmastide."

How could he seem so sure?

He shrugged. "Although, the family has other estates. It is possible they are not home."

Gabby's stomach flipped and not just because she hadn't eaten since afternoon. What if this Lord Brinton was not at home? Where would they go? And would they make it there in this weather without freezing to death? The bricks had long since lost their heat and there was little left of the rugs once they covered Katie and Sophia.

"Even if he is not at home, I am certain we can apply to the housekeeper for lodging, at least for tonight. No good Christian would turn us away in a storm such as this." There he was, sounding confident again.

Gabby knew that should make her feel better. But it didn't. She'd met plenty of people who claimed to be good Christians but treated their fellow men with disdain. She'd seen it plenty from the British soldiers who had lived just outside her village in France. Not all were brutes, but plenty were.

Then there was that man at the fair. He would undoubtedly claim to be a good Christian, and yet he'd spurned her just because she was from a country he had ill feelings for. No, she was not confident in the least that they would have proper shelter tonight.

The carriage turned slowly, the wheels slipping as it made the curve. Gabby clutched at her dress and closed her eyes until the carriage re-gripped the road.

What felt like an hour passed before the carriage stopped. The snow came down so fast it was difficult to see the house through the window of the carriage.

The door opened and Lord Kirtley stood, ducking out of the door. "Stay here while I inquire within. There is no need for all of us to wait in the blasted snow," he shouted over his shoulder.

Lady Kirtley gasped. "Hugh. Your language."

He glanced back at the children. "They are asleep, Eleanor. I have not corrupted them, at least not this time." He winked before he climbed from the carriage and pulled his greatcoat tightly around him. With his head down, he made his way up the steps, disappearing in the darkness and snow.

Gabby tried not to chew her lip. Lord Kirtley was certain things would be well. She needed to trust him. He'd never lied to her before, to her knowledge. Why should he do so now?

The carriage door opened, and he poked his head in. "It is just as I thought. We are welcome to stay at Ivydale for the time being." He held out his hand to Lady Kirtley. "Come, come. Let's get everyone inside and warm."

Lady Kirtley roused Winston and guided the sleepy boy toward his father. Then she followed behind. Lord Kirtley positioned the boy over his shoulder and held his hand out to his wife. As he handed her down, he shouted into the carriage, "Please get the other children up to the nursery. They are readying it as we speak."

Miss Carter and Nurse Jones waited for Gabby to stand before they moved to shift the girls into their arms. A footman handed Gabby down then turned to help the others from the carriage.

Gabby looked up at the front of the house. It was large. She dared say it was even bigger than Dovehaven, the Kirtleys' estate, although she would never utter such thoughts aloud.

The wind pulled at her bonnet, the ribbons whipping against her face. It was difficult to tell which stings came from the snow and which came from the slapping ribbon. She bent her head and hurried up the stairs and to the doorway.

The warmth of the house was a stark contrast to the cold outside. Gabby worked her jaw, the prickle of cold making the action painful in her cheeks.

A footman approached and asked for her coat. Gabby unbuttoned her pelisse and pulled on her ribbons, releasing her bonnet. She handed them over, only now taking the time to observe her surroundings.

The entry was wider than it was deep. Dark wood paneling lined the staircase which sat to one side, and white walls reached high above to the coved ceiling. Portraits of a lady and a man hung on the wall at the landing, as if watching to ensure no one went unseen. Yellow and blue marble tiles formed a pattern on the floor that was quite pleasing to the eye.

Gabby smiled. The house was elegant yet inviting.

"Ah, is everyone in then?" A deep, gravelly voice jerked her head around.

"I thought this was the home of Lord Brinton," Gabby whispered fiercely to Lord Kirtley.

"Yes, it is." Lord Kirtley smiled brightly, his hand extended. "I had not heard about the death of his brother. Mr. Campbell—you remember Mr. Campbell, do you not?—is the new Lord Brinton."

Gabby looked at the man walking down the stairs. It really *was* him.

"Brinton. It is good to see you again." Lord Kirtley pumped the man's hand. "Although, calling you Brinton will take some getting used to. I have no doubt I shall call you Campbell on more than one occasion."

Gabby's eyes widened. From the glance Lord Brinton tossed her way, he was no happier with her presence than she was with his. Gabby looked toward the doorway where the footman had disappeared with her coat. Perhaps she had been wrong. Freezing in the carriage seemed a perfectly acceptable option.

CHAPTER 4

Aaron folded the paper on his lap and took a sip of his tea. The rustling of skirts, however, had him unfolding it once more, just in case it happened to be the Frenchwoman. He folded down a corner and lifted his eyes. Rebekah stood in the doorway, her gaze darting around the room.

Aaron returned his eyes back to his paper. "Good morning, Lady Brinton. I hope you slept well."

"I did. Thank you, my lord." She moved to the sideboard and placed several things on her plate before setting it down on the table.

Aaron tilted his head to the side just enough to see that she was sitting across from him. Now why, with all the chairs at this table, would she sit directly across from him? It was not as if they knew each other well or had anything to discuss. "Come now. Are we not brother and sister? I believe it would be appropriate for you to call me Brinton."

She smiled eagerly, and he cleared his throat. "Or Aaron? Perhaps that would be best if you are comfortable with it." Now that he thought on it, *he* might be more comfortable with the latter. With people calling *him* Lord Brinton, it felt too intimate then to be called by the same name. It inferred a connection they did not have, nor did he want. Although, the notion of her calling him Aaron didn't settle all that well either.

"Good morning, Camp—Brinton." Lord Kirtley entered the breakfast room.

Aaron's body relaxed slightly. It did not appear an intimate conversation with Rebekah would happen, after all. He would have to thank Kirtley for the interruption. "How are you this morning, Kirtley?" Aaron grinned up at his old friend.

"Much better than we would have been in that carriage had you not taken us in." Kirtley placed a hand on Aaron's shoulder and squeezed. "I cannot thank you enough for your kindness."

"I am happy to have you here." His smile faltered. He was happy to have *most* of them there.

Lady Kirtley appeared in the doorway.

Aaron stood and bowed. "Lady Kirtley, how do you do? I hope you found your rooms acceptable."

She smiled prettily. It was no wonder Kirtley adored her—you could see it in his eyes whenever he looked upon his wife. "I could ask for nothing more, my lord. Thank you."

Aaron retook his seat, the realization that if Lord and Lady Kirtley were here, the *French* girl must soon follow. Perhaps a conversation with Lady Brinton was not so unappealing as he'd previously thought.

By the time he'd finished his second cup of tea, Aaron realized that perhaps he had been wrong about the French girl coming down.

Perhaps she was a late sleeper. He scoffed. Such behavior would not surprise him of her kind. His eyes narrowed at the thought of such indolent behavior.

Finally, he could not stand the anticipation of the impending unpleasantness. "And where is the young lady you brought with you? I hope she has not taken ill from the cold." He rested his paper in his lap, feigning interest.

"When I checked in on her this morning, she said she was well, and I'm inclined to believe her. Her cheeks had plenty of color in them." Lady Kirtley sopped up the sauce on her plate with a piece of bread.

"Then why has she not joined you for breakfast?" Why did he care? Was he not relieved she was not here?

"She said she wished to take breakfast in her room this morning." Lady Kirtley shrugged as if it was nothing to concern himself about.

Why would she take breakfast in her rooms if she was well? Was it him? Had she not wished to be in contact with him? He bristled. It felt personal. As if she were slighting him. But then, why should he expect any less from the French?

"I assume she will go up and eat with the children. I think she misses her time with them." Lady Kirtley smiled as if she found such behavior endearing.

Aaron nodded but did not reply. Had she been their governess? If so, why was she being treated now as if she was more than hired help?

He glanced out the window. It appeared to have stopped snowing, but the wind made it difficult to know for certain. "I am afraid you will not leave today. The roads are surely too slippery. I do not know if we will even be able to retrieve your carriage as yet."

Kirtley followed his gaze outside. "Yes, I was afraid that would be the case when I opened our curtains this morning. It is still frigid. It will keep the roads from being muddy, but the ice may not be any better."

"I hope you do not feel as though you need to leave immediately. I would welcome you to stay on through Twelfth Night, though I am sure you have plans for Christmastide." What was he saying? He truly would not mind having Kirtley and his family stay on for a fortnight. But if they stayed, Miss—he did not even remember her name, though he was certain Lady Kirtley had mentioned it last night—would stay on with them. Did he really want her in his house until Twelfth Night? He gripped the arms of his chair. It seemed too late for reservations. He couldn't very well retract the offer now.

"We have nothing so pressing as to risk traveling in this dreadful weather." Lady Kirtley wiped at her mouth with her serviette. "We thank you for your invitation and hospitality, my lord."

Aaron placed his paper on the table, scooting his chair back. "I have some papers to review in my study." He looked to Kirtley. "Please join me, if you are so inclined. I should rather enjoy hearing of your life these last years."

Kirtley's eyes brightened. "I am sure I would enjoy that. I have some letters I must send off and then I shall find you."

Aaron dipped a shallow bow. "Lady Kirtley. Lady Brinton." It felt more intimate to call his sister-in-law by her title—the name they now shared—than it would her Christian name, but she had not yet granted him that liberty.

He moved into his study and picked up the most recent ledger off the desk as he sat down behind it. Aaron had not been through all the books, but from what he had seen, his father and brother had both been good managers of the estate. Judging from some earlier ledgers, the coffers were full, although he'd never been privy to that information before, so he did not know if they could be more so. He still needed to visit the tenant cottages. Although, he doubted there was anything there worth his concern.

He opened the book and ran his index finger down the columns. The first harvest of the season last year had been good. But winter had come earlier than usual, and the second wheat crop had frozen before they could harvest it. It seemed the cherries had suffered a similar fate.

Aaron ran a hand through his hair. Because the estate had been managed well previously those losses were not so devastating as they could have been. He sat back and stared at the pages. But they could still be for the tenants. Was there anything he could do to help them?

He stretched his head to the side. Was he ready for this kind of responsibility? Steepling his fingers in front of his chin, he stared at the flames flickering in the grate across the room. He'd been responsible for the lives of dozens of men—perhaps even hundreds over the years

—while serving in the army. Surely managing an estate was not so stressful. It was not as if lives were at stake as they had been in France.

He pushed his chair back and stretched his legs out, crossing them at the ankles. It may not be lives he now held in his hands, but it was livelihoods, which could equate to the same thing, could it not? If he mismanaged this estate, people would lose the means of supporting their families—their homes. It was a position he did not take lightly.

He glanced at the mantel clock. Even if it were cold, his horse, Sargent, could make it to the far side of the estate where the tenant cottages were. It would give him a chance to see with his own eyes their condition. It would also give him some notion of what he could give his tenants for St. Stephen's Day.

He shook his head. He'd never thought he would need to worry about such things.

A knock sounded at his door. Kirtley was earlier than Aaron had expected him. He must have been very concise in his letters.

"Come."

The door pushed inward, but it was not Kirtley who entered. It was Lady Brinton. Oh, lud. What could she want?

"Lady Brinton." He cringed inwardly. "What brings you to my study this morning?" He watched as she turned and closed the door behind her. Now, why did she do that? The hairs on the back of his neck stood on end.

She moved noiselessly to the chair across from him. "I have wanted to speak with you."

Aaron slowly straightened, clasping his hands together on his desk. "How may I be of assistance?"

Rebekah swallowed and looked at her hands. "I wondered—that is—I am uncertain of what is to become of me."

Aaron turned his head slightly as if he had not heard her correctly. "What is to become of you? I do not understand your meaning."

"I am not the wife of a viscount anymore and I was not fortunate enough to have a son who would ensure my tenure in this house." She looked up and caught his gaze. "And so I ask you, what shall I expect? I have little jointure to live on and my father cannot accept me back in his house."

Aaron's brows rose. 'Pon rep, he'd not considered any of her concerns in the slightest. He furrowed his brow. "Your father is a vicar, is he not?"

She nodded. "He already has five children living at home. He thought himself rid of me—with a husband to care for me. But now..." Her breath came out as a flutter. She twisted at the lace on her sleeve.

"I confess, Lady Brinton. I have not thought on this. I had not realized it was a subject of concern." He licked his lips, and she stared intently at him, her face softening. Oh, lud. That was not what he'd been after. "Please, give me until Epiphany to come up with a solution."

She nodded. "I have an idea if you would like to hear it." She smiled coyly at him. Her demeanor having completely changed since her arrival at his study door.

"Thank you, but I believe I can discover a solution." She opened her mouth, and he cut her off. "However, if I find I am unable to find something suitable, be assured, I shall seek you out."

She nodded. "If you are in need of anything—"

"No." The word rang from his lips as he shot to his feet and strode around his desk. "I do not think that will be necessary. But thank you for your offer." He bowed to her, hoping she would take it as a dismissal because he wanted her out of his study. Now.

She read him correctly and stood, her face creased in a frown.

His stomach burned, and he tried to soften his words. "I understand your concern and I will make every effort for your continued comfort." He walked toward the corridor, yanking open the door. Kirtley stood just outside, his hand raised to knock.

"Kirtley." What would he think when he saw Lady Brinton leaving Aaron's study? Why had she insisted on shutting the door?

Kirtley grinned at Aaron and made to step inside until Lady Brinton appeared in his way. He stepped back. "Begging you pardon, my lady. I did not see you there." His eyes flicked to Aaron.

She brushed past them. "Thank you for your assistance, Aaron." She said a bit breathlessly.

Of course, now she would use his Christian name. Why had he told her that was permissible? Why did every name he had sound too informal when coming from her lips?

She hadn't needed to explain her plan to him. Her body language had told him all he needed to know. And he was *not* in agreement.

He frowned. At least he believed he knew her intent. But it *was* possible he was reading her wrong. *Lud, I hope I am.*

He dipped his head to Rebekah and motioned Kirtley in with a grand sweep of his arm. "Come in, Kirtley. It's been much too long since we've spoken." The earl stepped in and Aaron shut the door behind him, moving toward the sofa in front of the fireplace. "Would you care for a glass of brandy?"

Kirtley took a seat on the opposite couch. "Yes, thank you."

Aaron poured two glasses, taking one over and handing it to his friend. "It has been too long. While I enjoyed my time in the army, I find I have missed out on a great deal here at home." He grinned "For example, you seem most fortunate in your choice of a wife."

Kirtley barked out a laugh. "Yes, indeed. I could not have found a better match than Eleanor." His laughter subsided, turning into a soft smile instead.

Aaron's chest tightened. "I can tell from the looks you share that yours is a marriage of love." Was that envy in his voice? He hoped Kirtley had not heard it.

"I am fortunate. It does not always happen that you fall in love with the one that is best for you—at least not in the eyes of your father and the *Ton.*" Kirtley motioned to Aaron with his glass. "What of you, Camp...er, I am sorry, Brinton."

Aaron waved away his friend's apology. "Do not make yourself uneasy. I have difficulty remembering it myself."

Kirtley chuckled. "Yes, but you seem to have no problem calling me something different from when we were at Eton."

"Yes, well, we always knew you would become Lord Kirtley. While we called you Viscount Lislemont, in the back of our minds we called you Kirtley, even then." Aaron sucked in a deep breath. "Whereas I was never meant to be Viscount Brinton. It was never in the back of anyone's mind to call me such."

"You have my condolences. Henry was a good man."

Aaron ran a hand down his thigh. "Yes, he was." *And I am reminded of it daily.*

Kirtley grinned. "Have you been too busy fighting Napoleon to find yourself a wife?"

Aaron chortled. "I suppose that is the way of it." Now that he was home and settled as the Viscount Brinton, society—and his mother—would expect him to find a wife and start a family. Especially after Henry had died without an heir. The need for Aaron to have one would undoubtedly become something for his mother to latch hold of. He was rather surprised she had not begun the lectures already.

CHAPTER 5

Gabby climbed the stairs slowly toward the nursery. It had been months since she had spent any quality time with the children. Gabby was not a governess, after all. The voice in her head sounded remarkably similar to Lady Kirtley.

It was true, she was not a governess. But did it have to follow that she could not enjoy the children's company? Gabby had missed teaching them French and reading them stories—playing their silly little games. Even if it seemed to annoy Miss Carter.

Gabby had no siblings. Nor did she have any cousins—none that she knew of, anyhow. It was likely the reason she had taken instantly to Peter when he had come to live with them. While her father had always been attentive, it had been different having someone younger, more knowledgeable of society in this new century. Gabby grinned. Her father had never fully come out of the last one.

But even Peter could not serve the same function as a sister. And that is what Gabby had found the most endearing in the Kirtley nursery—Katie and Sophia. Two little sisters she had never known she needed. They were both far too young to discuss things such as gentlemen and the latest fashions—neither of which interested

Gabby overly much—but it had surprised her how much she had bonded with the little girls and so quickly.

Now that their time together was limited, Gabby realized just *how much* she needed them.

Gabby wrapped her arms around her middle, the coldness—open hostility, even—of their host, had enhanced the ever-growing feelings of loneliness even more. Gabby found herself almost desperate to spend time with her *sisters*. She even believed she could endure Winston's company for a time.

The door to the schoolroom was open a crack. She could hear Miss Carter speaking to Katie and Winston. Katie was visible as was half of Winston.

Gabby grinned as Katie bent her head to do as Miss Carter instructed, while Winston smirked and fiddled with his pencil. Miss Carter tapped her finger on his slate and whispered. Knowing Miss Carter, she uttered words of encouragement. The governess had not yet realized what Gabby had. Winston did not need coddling; he needed a firm hand and the enticement of fun if he did his assignments. It was amazing what the promise of ice skating could do for the boy.

Gabby had tried to explain as much to the governess, but Miss Carter had wanted none of Gabby's interference.

Winston grumbled.

A wail sounded from within the nursery and Gabby's chest tightened. Some time ago, Gabby would have been the one to fetch Sophia and comfort her until she fell back to sleep. The little girl must have awakened early from her nap. If she awoke naturally, she was a happy child. But if something awakened her, Hades himself would send Sophia back. The crying indicated the latter this time.

Gabby waited, listening for Nurse Jones to get the little girl, but Sophia continued to cry. Unable to stand it a moment longer, Gabby pushed through the door. "Where is Nurse Jones? Why is no one to fetch Sophia?"

Miss Carter raised a brow. "My job is these children, not the babe."

Gabby sighed and looked heavenward. Miss Carter had never been what Gabby would call a friend. "Where is Nurse Jones?" she asked again.

"She is below stairs." Miss Carter turned her attention back to Winston, who seemed perfectly content with the distraction.

"Very well. I shall see to Sophia." Gabby turned on her heel, but a moment of rebellion seized her, and she turned back. "Winston, if you finish your assignment for Miss Carter, I will take you ice skating. I have the perfect view of a little pond from my window."

Miss Carter glared at her, but Winston nodded and bent his head low, scribbling on his slate with new fervor.

Gabby bit the side of her cheek to keep from openly laughing and headed for the nursery door on the far side of the room. She twisted on the knob and slipped inside. Her heart swelled when the little girl lifted her arms up.

Gabby smiled and pulled Sophia to her, wrapping her arms around the small body. "Hello, kitten. I am here now. No need for tears."

She moved over to the rocker and settled Sophia on her lap, the girl's head resting on Gabby's chest. Stroking her silky hair, Gabby murmured quietly in Sophia's ear.

It did not seem to matter that the words were in French, Sophia quieted, her little body shuddering periodically from the bout of tears. Before long, the shudders turned to deep sighs and soft snores.

Gabby sang softly as she rocked back and forth, breathing in the scent of Sophia's hair, mixed with the saltiness of perspiration brought on by her fit of tears.

The door swung open soundlessly on its hinges and Nurse Jones stepped lightly into the room. She smiled at Gabby, mouthing her thanks for Gabby's help.

Gabby nodded. It was times like this when she questioned if it would be so terrible to be a governess or nurse. She had never felt such unconditional love as she had from this child. But Lady Kirtley had assured Gabby that there was no need for her to settle for such a life. Peter had ensured that Gabby had a sizeable dowry, ensuring an advantageous marriage. Or so Lady Kirtley believed. Gabby, however, had her doubts.

Nurse Jones gathered several things from the room before leaving Gabby alone with Sophia.

The little girl shifted in Gabby's arms and she knew she should lay her back down in bed. Gabby sighed. The last thing she wanted to do was abandon Sophia. If she did, it would require her to find something else to occupy her time. After her little stunt with Winston, it was doubtful Miss Carter would be obliged to cut the lesson short today. Besides, it was the first time in weeks Gabby had felt needed—felt wanted—and she was reluctant to let it end.

A throat cleared in the doorway and Gabby looked up smiling, expecting to see Nurse Jones. Instead, Lord Brinton stood in the doorway, his perpetual frown firmly in place. "Ah, here you are." He did not lower his voice in the least. Did he not notice the child asleep on her lap?

Sophia shifted.

Gabby raised a brow and pulled the girl tighter to her, placing her hand over Sophia's ear. "Yes, here I am," she whispered, then looked down at the little girl in her lap. Surely, Lord Brinton would understand the hint.

"I have been looking for you, Miss..." He did not lower his voice until he trailed off upon realizing he did not know her name. That *was* why he had not used it, was it not? Had she ever heard him call her by name? "No one seemed to know where you were."

Gabby narrowed her eyes. Was he daft or did he wish to wake a sleeping child? "I am here," she whispered fiercely. Maybe if she emphasized the whisper, he would figure out that he should whisper also. "What ees it zat you need?"

He reared back.

A part of her wanted to speak with an even thicker accent if only to see how he would react. But she'd already acted out of rebellion once today. Additionally, she knew that Lady Kirtley would frown on such an action and think it childish. Gabby pushed the urge down. She did not want to disappoint Eleanor. Sometimes Gabby forgot how fortunate she was that Peter had brought her here. She looked around. Not here, per se, but to England.

"A group of us are going in search of greenery to decorate for Christmastide. Lady Kirtley thought you may enjoy coming along." His voice was dull.

Gabby ran a finger down the side of Sophia's face. Was the fact that Lord Brinton had deliberately mentioned it was not his idea significant? Was he implying something—letting her know that he cared so little for her that he had not thought to include her? Gabby didn't know why that disappointed her, but it did. "She was correct; I should love to come. Are we to leave immediately?"

"You have a few minutes before you need to meet the others."

She didn't miss that he had emphasized *you*. He was obviously trying to dissuade her from using *we*, as if it assumed too much intimacy regarding the two of them. She looked to the ceiling. What a ridiculous man he was.

Gabby nodded. "I just need to lay Sophia down and change into something warmer."

He nodded and turned to leave, but not before giving her a long look. What did he mean by it?

She lifted a shoulder. He was likely just discovering something else about her which was lacking.

She placed Sophia in the bed and placed a quick kiss on the girl's forehead before hurrying to her own room. Aline helped her change into her thick wool dress and her sturdy boots. She hoped the snow was not so deep it would come up over and fall inside. She shivered just thinking about the wetness running down her ankles.

Gabby took her bonnet from Aline. "Please keep zee fire stoked, Aline. I am certain I shall be chilled through by zee time we return."

Her maid smiled and dipped her head. "Yes, miss."

Looking at the clock on the mantel, Gabby placed a hand to her mouth. "Oh, zat took longer zan expected." She hurried from the room and down the stairs.

Lord Kirtley and Lord Brinton stood at the bottom in the entryway, greatcoats over their arms and their beavers in hand.

Lord Brinton thumped the top of his hat on the palm of his hand, his irritation in her lateness clear.

"Miss Babineaux. I'm glad you are to join us." Lord Kirtley spoke her name overly loud.

Gabby stared at him.

"Yes, Miss Babineaux, we are glad you are to join us." Lord Brinton repeated, sounding anything but excited. He glanced at Lord Kirtley and then back at her. "I hope you have dressed warmly."

"Zees is my warmest dress. But I have instructed Aline to keep zee fire stoked so my room will be warm when I return." She was slightly gratified by the twitch in Lord Brinton's cheek.

A footman appeared from a side room carrying her pelisse and gloves. He bowed and held them out to her.

Lord Kirtley nudged Lord Brinton and he stepped forward. "Please, allow me." Lord Brinton took her coat and held it up for her.

Gabby did not miss the scowl he threw to Lord Kirtley as she turned away from them and slipped her arms in.

She looked at him from over her shoulder. "Zank you."

"You are welcome." This gentleman had a way of making even the most pleasant of phrases sound distasteful.

He walked away from her without another word, collecting his things from Lord Kirtley.

Lady Brinton cleared her throat from the top of the stairs, and all eyes turned in her direction. She smiled, her gaze resting on Lord Brinton.

Gabby looked back over her shoulder. She was uncertain what was happening between Lord Brinton and his sister-in-law. But when she looked to him, his attention was on Lord Kirtley.

Gabby's brows hitched a notch. Interesting. Whatever was happening, it looked to be on the part of Lady Brinton only.

Lady Brinton glided down the stairs. The footman brought out her coat and held it up for her to slip into. She cleared her throat again. "Aaron, would you be so kind as to help me with my pelisse?"

"Of course, Lady Brinton." Gabby grinned. It appeared she was not the only person in this house to earn Lord Brinton's irritations and colorless tone of voice. Although why that made Gabby happy, she was not certain.

He passed his coat back into Lord Kirtley's arms and stepped to help Lady Brinton.

Lady Kirtley raced down the stairs, much faster than Gabby would have thought proper. It was refreshing to see the proper lady do something so wholly improper from time to time.

Lady Kirtley sighed, shoving her hands into her gloves. "I do apologize, Hugh. A button fell off just as we were finishing dressing. But this cold is hard on Heath's fingers. They stiffen up so much she can scarcely hold the needle."

Lord Kirtley held his wife's pelisse. "Perhaps it's time to find a new maid, Elea—"

Lady Kirtley held up a hand. "No, Hugh. Do not even mention it. I will hear no more on the subject. Heath has been with my family for years."

Gabby leaned into Lady Kirtley, grateful that she was not willing to entertain such a notion. "You are welcome to ask Aline for help if you are in need of needlework again. She would be happy to help."

Lady Kirtley took Gabby's hand and patted it. "Thank you, Gabrielle. I shall inform Heath when we return."

Lord Brinton finally shrugged into his own coat. "Shall we be on our way? We do not have far to go, but in this weather, I'm afraid it will feel as if we have to go all the way to the continent, at the very least."

"I know the best places to find the mistletoe for the kissing balls."

Lady Brinton smiled at Lord Brinton. Was she fluttering her lashes at him?

Gabby watched in fascination.

His face pinked, but he returned the smile with his own wooden, forced one. He motioned to the front doors. "Perhaps it would be best if we divide into groups. It will save time and hopefully keep us from freezing or at the very least, catching a cold."

Lady Brinton stood close to Lord Brinton. "What a lovely idea. Shall we be partners?"

He took a step away.

Gabby stepped forward. "Lady Brinton, I was hoping I could go with you. I have seen the lovely winter garden from my window, and I'd hoped someone could show it to me."

Lady Brinton flicked her gaze to Lord Brinton, then returned them to Gabby. "There is no mistletoe in the winter garden. We must go to the far side of the woods to find it."

Lord Brinton motioned to Lord and Lady Kirtley. "Lady Brinton, I think it best if you go with Lord and Lady Kirtley to gather the mistletoe and holly. They do not know the estate and will need your guidance to know where to go. I will go with Miss Babineaux and Paul." He motioned for a footman to join them. "We will gather the bay branches and the yew from the winter garden." He rubbed his hand up and down his arm and looked just over Lady Brinton's shoulder. "I sent Jacobs to the forest this morning to cut us some evergreen branches." He grinned, but Gabby knew it was meant for everyone but her. And perhaps Lady Brinton. "I think we shall have a nice assortment of colors and smells."

He placed his hand on the small of Gabby's back and gave her a small nudge forward. She stumbled slightly, the warmth of his hand moving up her spine and into her chest. She chided herself. Surely it was just the added heat his hand provided. They hated each other, did they not? And enemies did not relish the feel of the other's touch. It most certainly could not be excitement she was feeling, which left only the added heat on this cold winter day as the reason for her reaction.

"Ready, Miss Babineaux?" Lord Brinton's voice held a hint of excitement. Was he looking forward to being with her? A guttural sound rushed from her throat at the unlikeliness of it.

He cast a glance over at her and sighed. That is when she realized his excitement had more to do with him *not* being with Lady Brinton.

CHAPTER 6

Aaron trudged back to the house with Miss Babineaux at his side. He was mildly impressed that she could keep up with his long strides. His toes felt nearly frozen; he could only assume hers were as well.

Paul walked behind them, the bundle of branches slung over his shoulder in a large piece of canvas.

He and Miss Babineaux made their way up the front steps while Paul veered around to the side of the house. Their outing had been a rather quiet one, not that Aaron had minded. His thoughts kept turning to what he had witnessed in the nursery. As much as he wished to shake the memory, it would not leave his mind. Miss Babineaux, with a child sleeping comfortably on her lap, singing softly as she rocked.

Aaron frowned. It was not a memory he could reconcile with his opinions of the lady. Mireille would surely never have done something so tender, so...

Aaron shook his head with a low growl. It was likely a ploy by Miss Babineaux to make him see her differently. Only, her ploy would not work. He was not so easily fooled—at least not this time.

The normally cool entry felt hot to his cold nose and cheeks, the feeling of tiny pinpricks bringing instant discomfort. He looked over to see Miss Babineaux working her mouth and rubbing at her cheeks.

"Ah, Aaron. There you are. I expected you back before now." Lady Brinton hurried across the entryway, placing her hand on his arm. "We had much farther to go and still made it back before you." She flicked her gaze to Miss Babineaux. "Pray, what took you so long?" Her voice held a possessive quality Aaron did not appreciate.

Aaron stepped back, causing her hands to drop away. She cast her eyes downward and he felt a tug of guilt. "We had to dig the bay branches out of the snow. I knew the general area, but with no precise location, there was much digging. It took longer than expected." He took off his greatcoat and handed it over to Marcus, the footman assigned to the entryway. "Besides, you had the sled at your disposal. Walking takes much longer."

"We found the mistletoe and holly without a problem." Lord Kirtley's voice boomed as he came through the doorway at the other side of the entry. "Lady Brinton knew just where to look."

Aaron's mother followed Kirtley through the door. "There you are, Aaron. We were about to believe you lost." She motioned for him to come closer. "It *has* been some time since you were here. I thought you might not remember where to go. Henry always knew just where to find the yew. If he were here, I'm sure we would be well on our way to completing this task."

Aaron breathed in deeply through his nose, kneading at the knots in his neck. "I am certain that is true, Mother."

Kirtley glanced at him, his brows raised.

Aaron looked away. He did not need to bother his friend with his frustrations. "How may I help, Mother, so we might complete this chore in a timely manner?"

She sighed. "If you think it a chore, Aaron, then perhaps it would be better if you did not help. This is tradition and it's intended to be fun."

A corner of his mouth quirked up. Yes, her tone certainly *indicated* great joy and entertainment. "Begging your pardon."

His mother looked at the bundles gathered on the canvas, now laying on the floor. "Lady Brinton, perhaps you and Aaron could work on the greenery for the staircase."

Aaron opened his mouth to protest, but Miss Babineaux spoke first. "I should love to work with Lady Brinton. Decorating zee stairs was always my assignment at home."

Aaron stared at her. What was she doing? This was the second time today the lady had tried to align herself with Rebekah. Aaron could see it was just another ploy, but to what end? What could she hope to gain by earning Rebekah's good opinion?

"I had thought to do the kissing balls, my lady." Rebekah flicked her glance over to Aaron.

He looked away. Frustration surged through him. What was wrong with Rebekah? At every turn, she flirted and fluttered her lashes at him. The notion Aaron had misread her earlier, all but gone now.

Henry, in all his letters, had never once mentioned his wife's tendency to flirt. Indeed, he spoke of her in the opposite.

Was she thinking he would make an offer to her? Marry his brother's widow? In the eyes of God—and Aaron, for that matter—Rebekah was his sister. She was mistaken if she thought a union between them possible.

His mother shrugged. "Very well." She motioned to the table at the far end of the hall that Aaron only now noticed. His mother must have had it moved here while they'd been out collecting the greenery.

"Aaron, perhaps you would be good enough to help Miss Babineaux with the staircase?" His shoulders relaxed, even as Rebekah's head dropped. Why was he relieved to be working with the Frenchwoman? He despised everything about her. He squinted at her. Well, perhaps he did not despise her eyes. They were pleasant enough to look at.

His mother's voice brought him back to the moment.

"Then once Lady Brinton has completed the kissing balls, you and Lord Kirtley could hang them?"

Aaron dipped his head, hoping he heard everything his mother had said. "As you wish, Mother."

He moved over to where Miss Babineaux stood next to the staircase, her hands clasped in front of her. He supposed listening to her infuriating accent was better than enduring the longing looks of Lady Brinton.

"Miss Babineaux, it appears we are to be partners for the next few hours." He stared up the long banister. "Perhaps longer." He shifted his gaze back to her. "I have little knowledge of what to do; I hope you did not exaggerate your experience, or we shall be here the whole of the day."

She smiled, and he decided her eyes were not her only redeeming quality. "Our staircases at home were not so vast as zis, but we *did* have a staircase. I believe I know what to do."

Aaron relaxed. "Very good. Tell me what I am to do."

His mother came over. "Aaron, do you have any notion of what you are doing here?" She reached for branches of several varieties. She bunched them together and tied them with a string. Shoving the bundle into his hands she motioned to the railing. "Now tie it to the staircase with ribbon. I'm certain Miss Babineaux can tie a proper bow, can you not?" His mother looked to the young lady and made the motions of tying the ribbon into a bow.

Aaron grinned. Apparently, his mother did not believe Miss Babineaux understood enough English to know what his mother was saying. Would the lady be offended?

Miss Babineaux grinned. "Oui—yes, my lady." She flicked her eyes over to Aaron.

"Very good. Carry on." His mother waved her hand at the greenery and walked away.

Aaron carried the bundle in his hand over the stairs and Miss Babineaux followed behind with the ribbon. She unwound several lengths from the spool and tied it around the greenery.

They worked together, neither saying anything.

Only Miss Babineaux's humming drifted through the entry hall as they bundled and tied, over and over again. She had a pleasant tone to her voice, and he found he rather enjoyed listening to it. Most of the songs he recognized as Christmas carols and he hummed along with her, the spirit of Christmastide overcoming him.

Perhaps his mother had been correct. This was an enjoyable activity. Curious he'd never thought so in the past. That he was finding it so while here with *this Frenchwoman*—his nose curled even thinking the word—who he had no friendly inclinations toward, was disquieting. It truly must be the spirit of Christmastide.

"Zee first staircase eez done. Shall we move up to zee next floor?"

Aaron nodded. "Yes, I am certain Lady Brinton is creating kissing balls as quickly as she can."

Miss Babineaux looked at him curiously but said nothing as she gathered an armful of their greenery bundles and moved to the stairs.

Aaron wished the words back. They had made him sound arrogant. It was not as if he thought every woman desired his attentions. But surely Miss Babineaux had noticed Lady Brinton's flirtations. If she had, would she still consider him arrogant? It was possible his comments only increased the arrogance she already believed him to possess. He had not been very humble in his dealing with her thus far.

He bent and picked up the remaining bundles, climbing the steps behind her. She already thought very little of him, given the way he'd treated her. She must think even less of him now. But why did he care? She was French—*a grenouille*. Why was he desirous of her good opinion? He grunted, not liking the thought that he desired anything from Miss Babineaux.

He reached the landing and stacked the bundles on top of the ones she had brought.

Miss Babineaux was already working at fastening the first bundle on the railing. It slipped to one side, only to fall to the other side after she righted it. She huffed out a breath, a few wisps of hair blowing off her brow.

"Let me hold that while you fasten it." Aaron stepped over, grasping the greenery as he'd done with the bundles on the lower stairs.

"Sank you." Her voice was soft, and he leaned closer to hear her. The scent of roses mingled with the bay and evergreen. It was a pleasant scent.

"You are welcome." His voice came out softer than he had intended.

She looked up at him as if assessing his sincerity. She seemed surprised by what she saw.

In truth, he was a little taken aback himself when he realized he was, indeed, sincere. "Miss Babineaux, where in France"—he spit out the country's name— "are you from?"

She glanced up from the ribbon in her hand, studying him. It was a look he was coming to know. She did not open her mouth without taking a measure of him first. "Lyon."

What had she seen? It must not have been good if she kept her answer to only a single word.

"I've traveled through Lyon. It is a lovely city."

She nodded.

Hmm. Maybe they should just go back to the humming.

"I miss Lyon very much. But I'm coming to love England also. Warwickshire is a particular favorite."

Aaron's brows rose. So she could speak more than a single word. He'd almost wondered if that was all she was capable of. "Is there a reason you are partial to that shire?"

She shrugged. "It ees where Peter—er, Lord and Lady Rockwell live. I've visited zem with Lord and Lady Kirtley several times since coming to England."

He knew Lord Rockwell. It only now dawned on him that Lady Kirtley was Peter's sister. It made sense that they should visit Warwickshire. But there was a certain reverence—or maybe it was fondness—in Miss Babineaux's voice when she mentioned Peter. It had not escaped Aaron's notice that she called him Peter before correcting herself.

Aaron held onto a bundle as she secured it. "What brought you to England?"

She did not reply at first. After several beats, she looked up at him. "My father died and eet was determined zat I should come to England where Pet—" She stomped her foot and Aaron felt a slight flutter in his gut. "Lord Rockwell could provide for me."

Aaron stepped back. Why should such a task fall to Rockwell?

She must have sensed his question because she continued on. "Lord Rockwell lived with my father and me for more zan a year when I was a girl. My father was already three and fifty at zee time. He knew zee chances of him living to see me married were not in his favor. I had no other relatives. When my father died, I would be alone in zee world. My father asked Peter if when zat time came, I could come to England and live under his protection." She twisted at the end of a ribbon. "Zat time came a few years ago."

Lud. What a huge responsibility for Rockwell to take on. Aaron didn't know whether to praise the man or check to see if he'd taken leave of his senses. "You had no other relatives? What of your mother's family?"

"My mother's family disinherited her when she married my father. But even so, *la Républiquec* and *le Guillotine* made sure my mother could never make amends."

Aaron's mouth formed an O. He'd not encountered anyone with such close associations to the revolution before. Could it be she had no more love for Napoleon and his kind than Aaron did? "If Rockwell made the promise, why are you here with Lord and Lady Kirtley?"

She sighed. "When I came, Peter had not yet married. Even though I had not yet come out, neither he nor Lady Kirtley thought it proper for me to live wiz him." She grunted. "Even though we look on each other as brother and sister, zey deemed it best for me to live with Lord and Lady Kirtley."

"But Rockwell *is* married now." Why would she continue on with Lord and Lady Kirtley when it was obvious she preferred Rockwell?

"By zee time Lord and Lady Rockwell married, I'd already lived with his sister for some time. She thought it best for my situation to remain the same."

"But you would prefer to be with Lord and Lady Rockwell?"

She shook her head and smiled up at him, but it did not quite reach her eyes. "Of course not. Lord and Lady Kirtley have been very good to me. I am very grateful to zem." She pulled out several lengths of the ribbon and hurriedly tied it around the bundle he was holding. "I would miss Katie and Sophia." She made a face. "I believe I would even miss Winston. Besides, Lady Kirtley will sponsor me for zee next Season in London."

Interesting. "Rockwell is providing for you? Did your father not leave you an inheritance of some kind? Not even a dowry?"

She bristled. "Yes, my papa left me a dowry. It is not much." She bit her bottom lip. "But he was a good man, a good papa."

Aaron nearly smacked his hand to his head at his stupidity. He'd not intended to imply the man was not a good provider. Although, based on his past treatment of her, he could understand that she would instantly think he meant the worst.

He'd never heard of such an arrangement and was simply fascinated by the details of it. He held his hand up. "I am sorry if I gave you the impression I did not approve of your father. I am certain he was a good man, or Rockwell would never have agreed to take you in." He placed another bundle of greenery on the handrail.

She moved it slightly farther up and secured it. "He was a good man. Peter reminds me of him. So maybe it is good I do not live with him and Lady Rockwell in Warwickshire. It would make me miss Papa too much." Her tone said she did not agree.

"A small dowry will make for a difficult Season. I'm sure you have many desirable attributes, but—"

"I said my papa *left me* a small dowry. I did not say I *had* a small dowry." She narrowed her eyes at him. "I intend to do well zis Season."

Ah. Rockwell had added to her dowry as part of his *providing* for her. "Does Rockwell provide everything or do Lord and Lady Kirtley contribute as well?"

She glared at him. "I did not zink it proper for strangers to speak of such matters."

Aaron grimaced. She was correct. He was completely out of line to be asking such questions. "I apologize; I let my curiosity override my manners."

She gave him another appraising look. "You are forgiven, my lord." She eyed the last set of stairs. "Perhaps if we talk less, we can finish more quickly."

Aaron smiled at the less than subtle hint that he should stop talking to her. The problem was, now he didn't want to.

CHAPTER 7

Gabby stomped the snow from her boots as she stepped into the church. Her breath hovered in a cloud in front of her face. It was not significantly warmer inside than it was out, but at least it was not windy. She took consolation in that fact.

"What a lovely little church." Lady Kirtley clasped her hands together as she looked around.

"This is St. Francis Church. It dates back to Henry the fifth. A fire destroyed the main house in the late sixteen hundreds, but the third Viscount Brinton rebuilt it a short time later. But all this is mostly original." Lord Brinton spoke with pride in his voice, as if he, himself, had placed every stone they now looked at. He leaned forward slightly. "What do you think of our little church, Miss Babineaux?" His voice had lowered, allowing only her to hear.

The curl at the side of her face danced in his breath and she shivered.

"Are you still cold?" he asked.

She shrugged. "A little. But I am certain I will warm up now we are out of zee wind." Gabby took a step away from him. His manners and tone of voice had been kinder, or rather more polite today than since she had arrived. She did not know what to make of the change. Was it something she had said or done? Or was it merely a result of the Christmas spirit that seemed to be filling them all? Perhaps tomorrow they would return to interactions colored by distrust and disdain.

Lady Brinton sidled up beside him and wrapped her hands around his arm. "We should move to our bench, Aaron. It looks as though the vicar is waiting to start."

Lord Brinton lifted his arm discreetly away from her and turned to his mother. "Come, Mother. I do not want you left behind."

Lady Brinton cast her gaze downward as his mother scowled at him. "You need not treat me like an errant child, Aaron. I will be along." The dowager continued chatting with Mrs. Rivers, waving her son away.

He placed his hand at the small of Gabby's back and gave her a small nudge forward. Tingles and heat shot out in every direction traveling into her legs and arms, causing her to stumble on seemingly nothing. Lord Brinton moved his hand from her back and placed it at her waist, his other hand on her arm. "Are you well?"

Gabby nodded, unable to make a sound. She did not know if it was her near fall or Lord Brinton's closeness that made her mute. They walked several steps, the two of them so close it would have been difficult to determine they were two people, were it not for the difference in their clothing.

"The Brinton family bench is the third one from the front on the left side." Again, he whispered in her ear, and again, she shivered.

She clutched the ribbons of her reticule in her fist, angry at every raised bump on her skin. When would she learn to control herself when he did such things? Surely this was what Lady Kirtley was alluding to when she spoke of decorum. What if people thought there was partiality between the two of them? Or would they guess it was only on Gabby's part? She scowled at the greenery fastened to the bench. She did not have feelings for this man. Childish fancies did not constitute true feelings, after all.

Gabby walked down the aisle, looking up at the stain-glassed depictions of several saints. Perhaps if she studied them hard enough, those around them would simply think she was interested in them and they would not look any closer. But try as she may, she was simply unable to fully appreciate them as Lord Brinton continued to nudge her down the aisle.

He reached out a hand and pulled her to a stop at the row behind the one with the engraved marker bearing the Brinton name. Lord Brinton motioned Lady Brinton into the row first. She smiled up at him, reaching for his arm to pull him in after her. He turned and feigned a looked behind him, and her hand fell back to her side. Lady Brinton had missed the mark with Lord Brinton yet again.

Gabby looked away when the lady huffed.

"I thought I heard someone call out my name," Lord Brinton said as he returned his attention to the row. "I must have been mistaken." Motioning Gabby in next, he followed in behind her.

She moved forward but paused a few steps in from the aisle and looked up at him.

He flicked his gaze from her to Lady Brinton and back to her. Her lips turned up slightly, and he winked? What was that all about? She shook her head. Christmas did odd things to this man.

She moved the rest of the way into the bench, sitting down next to Lady Brinton.

Nurse Jones, Miss Carter, and the children settled on the bench behind them. Sophia reached forward and grabbed hold of Gabby's sleeve. Gabby gently unfisted the little girl's hand and turned around. "Be a good girl for Nurse Jones, Soph."

The little girl reached forward. "Babby."

Gabby kissed her fingers and placed them to the little girl's forehead. "If you are quiet for ze service, I will sing you a song before you rest." She flicked her eyes up to Nurse Jones for approval. The woman smiled and nodded. Unlike Miss Carter, Nurse Jones did not seem bothered by Gabby's presence in the nursery. Perhaps it was because she had never had dreams of having her own house, as Miss Carter did.

Lord Brinton settled in next to Gabby.

Her stomach fluttered, and her brow furrowed, all thoughts of Sophia fleeing her brain. Why could she not control herself better? Perhaps it was because he no longer seemed to glower at her every time he looked at her.

Lady Brinton stiffened beside her and the already cold church chilled a little more.

Suddenly the lady stood and lifted a hand. "Oh, I just saw Mrs. Davenport. I've been needing to speak to her. I shall be right back." She shimmied her way past Gabby and Lord Brinton's legs.

Lord Brinton's brows rose, even as his jaw tightened.

Lord and Lady Kirtley had yet to sit down, standing near the aisle speaking in low tones to a man Gabby did not know. They all leaned back slightly, giving Lady Brinton room to exit the bench.

Gabby's lip curved at the corners as she recognized the look of disapproval on Lady Kirtley's face.

Lord Brinton shrugged. "Perhaps we should scoot down. Lady Brinton will have to take the seat on the end, next to my mother." Gabby moved to the end of the bench by the wall. Now that she was seated—and Lord Brinton was not touching her—she could really look at the windows and the architecture of the building. She did not have the passion for design that her father did, but she could still appreciate a flying buttress. She smiled at the thought of her papa. He would surely have mentioned the changes *he* would have made had he designed this little church.

She took in a deep breath, allowing the smell and the feeling of this place to settle over her. This place felt like home—or at least like the church she used to attend in Lyon. It was the first time in a long while that she had felt as if she belonged.

"Pardon me, but I must get back to my seat." Lady Brinton whisper-talked to Lord and Lady Kirtley. Without waiting for a reply, she shimmied her way into the bench. Lady Kirtley's eyes went wide as the lady's backside passed in front of their faces.

Gabby's face heated in mortification. Surely the lady had better manners than this? The intake of breath from the dowager viscountess indicated she had thought the Lady better bred.

Lady Brinton wiggled her way onto the bench nearly sitting on Lord Brinton and Lord Kirtley's laps. "Perhaps it is best if I just sit here, rather than moving all the way in." She smiled down at Lord Kirtley but saved her biggest smile for Lord Brinton. "Can you believe I was not even able to speak with Mrs. Davenport?" Her head shook in disbelief.

Lord Kirtley scooted, making room for Lady Brinton. Once settled in his new location, he leaned forward, looking past Lady Brinton, and stared at his friend with slightly raised brows. His mouth twisted to one side and he nodded ever so slightly before sitting back.

Gabby knew that look. It was the one that indicated he did not know whether to laugh or be irritated. While Gabby did not look for confirmation, she could feel the whole of the church staring at Lord and Lady Brinton.

Lord Brinton must have felt it too because his thumb repeatedly bounced up and down on his thigh as his jaw worked furiously. Gabby even thought she heard him growl when his mother and Lord and Lady Kirtley shuffled down to make room next to Aaron.

Lady Brinton smiled her thanks to Lord Kirtley then turned and patted Lord Brinton's arm. She scooted closer to him, a feat Gabby did not think possible.

Gabby did not miss the subtle shift of Lady Brinton's leg as it hugged up close to his, nor did she miss Lord Brinton's stiff posture.

The service started and so did Lord Brinton's measured breathing. He clasped his hand tightly in his lap, his gloves pulled taut over his knuckles.

Lady Brinton seemed oblivious to his discomfiture. She sat with her hand tucked in the crook of his arm, smiling up at the vicar as he preached the Christmas sermon.

By the time the last amen was uttered, it was Gabby's leg that was touching Lord Brinton's as he endlessly shifted away from Lady Brinton. At one point she had half-expected him to move to her lap. She would have been angry or maybe excited—she wasn't sure which—at his forwardness, but she knew he was trying to disentangle himself from Lady Brinton. It meant nothing, even though she found herself delightfully warm—the center of that warmth radiating from her thigh.

When the vicar turned from the congregation, Aaron shot to his feet, his gaze roving the crowd, as if looking for the fastest means of escape.

Gabby felt sorry for the man. She didn't know much about Lady Brinton—only that she'd been married to Lord Brinton's brother and was now a young widow—but that information did not explain her very odd behavior.

The dowager cast a dark look down the bench at Lady Brinton and then up to her son before she stood and moved into the aisle.

The Kirtley's followed close behind her.

Lady Brinton stood and moved out of the bench, waiting in the aisle.

Lord Brinton sighed deeply before offering Gabby a hand up. She took it and stood behind him, waiting for him to move out with the rest of their party. But he stayed, blocking her from leaving.

"Excuse me, my lord. Are you waiting for somezing?" She bent slightly to look under their bench.

He shook his head. "No. We can go." He moved toward the aisle but stopped. "I must apologize. You must think me very untoward. I did not maintain a proper distance during the service. It is just..." His voice trailed off, and he rubbed a hand across the back of his neck.

"I understand, my lord. You need not apologize." She glanced toward the end of the bench to Lady Brinton, the only member of their party still waiting there. The others had moved down the aisle, smiling and nodding to people they passed. "It is she who owes *you* an apology."

He gave her a half-smile, and she took it for what it was—a thank you of sorts.

They moved the rest of the way to the aisle.

Lady Brinton looked expectantly at his arm. His face was a stony mask as he held out his arm to Lady Brinton and she smiled triumphantly until he offered his other arm to Gabby. Then the lady's smile dropped away.

They walked out into the cold, and Gabby found she welcomed the bite. At least it was a diversion from the frostiness vibrating off Lord Brinton. Relieved that for once, his stony glare was not directed at her, Gabby glanced over at Lady Brinton. Her stomach clenched and burned. She knew what Lady Brinton must be feeling.

Several flakes fell from the sky and Gabby squinted, the wind burning her eyes. She dropped Lord Brinton's arm, wrapping her pelisse tighter around her body. They did not have far to walk, but in this cold, it felt like miles. She quickened her steps, not sure why the rest of them seemed content to take a more leisurely pace. Did they not feel the biting cold?

As the house grew larger, she hurried faster, lifting her skirts and running the last several rods to the front steps. When the front door opened, she welcomed the burning that stung her cheeks and grudgingly handed her pelisse off to the footman. Bounding up the stairs in a most unladylike fashion, Gabby grinned. Lady Kirtley and the rest of the party had not yet made it back from the church. Gabby could slide down the banister for all they would know. But she did not, contenting herself with the race up the stairs.

Aline would have the fire stoked and Gabby could scarcely wait to settle into a chair to read or stitch. She did not care what she did, as long as she could be alone. She planned to sit for the rest of the afternoon, or at least until her feet thawed out.

She threw open her bedchamber door, and the heat hit her like a wall. Gabby sighed, letting the warmth envelope her like a blanket. "*Ah, mademoiselle. Est-ce que la messe vous a plu?*"

"English, Aline. You will never master it if you do not practice. Besides, it helps me to learn it as well."

"Oui—yes, miss." Aline moved toward the dressing screen. "Why could you not have moved to Bavaria or Hanover? I am more proficient in the Germanic languages." She huffed. "Even Italian would have been better."

Gabby snickered. "But think of the opportunities, Aline." She sighed. "Perhaps when I have children, I will make you a governess instead of my maid. Then you could teach my children all the languages you know."

There was a spark in Aline's eyes. "Are you in earnest, miss?"

Gabby grinned. "Only if you get better at your English. My children will be English, first and foremost." That thought brought a pang of homesickness to her chest. "It is likely their father will speak only English. So will the children. How will you teach them these other languages if you do not know their primary language?"

Aline nodded. "I will try harder, miss."

Gabby settled into the chair. "I know you will, Aline. I have complete faith in you."

Gabby thought she saw a hint of wetness in her maid's eyes.

"And yes, I enjoyed the service." She frowned. Had she even heard the service? Now that she thought on it, she could not recall a single thing the vicar had said. What she *did* remember was the feel of Lord Brinton's leg against hers and his hand as it sat on her waist. Her face heated. Such things a lady should not dwell on. He had only placed his hand there to keep her from falling.

Gabby leaned back in the chair, dropping her head and closing her eyes. She must stop thinking as if they were courting. They were not even friends. There had been a moment or two while they were decorating the staircase when it had felt like they could be. But those were isolated events where talking had felt necessary.

Aline helped Gabby change from her thick woolen dress into a lighter weight gown, more suitable for time indoors. As Aline fastened the last button, a knock sounded. Gabby's breath hitched. Could it be Lord Brinton?

It was not Lord Brinton—what a silly notion for her to think—but rather Lady Kirtley who stepped through the door. Gabby sighed. Her time alone was not to be—at least not until Lady Kirtley said what she came to say.

CHAPTER 8

Gabby poked her head out into the corridor and when no one was within view, she slipped out of her room.

After Lady Kirtley's short visit to check on her well-being, she'd done well staying in her rooms since returning from church. Neither Lord nor Lady Brinton had seemed amiable when the sermon had concluded and Gabby had not been interested in discovering if their moods had improved. But she had finished her books—many times over since arriving in England—and she wished for something else to do.

She made her way to the nursery. She had promised Sophia a song, and it was about time for her to rest for the afternoon. She pushed inside. The schoolroom appeared empty at first glance. But then she spied the corner with the settee and the bookshelves. Katie and Winston sat with Miss Carter, each with a book in their lap. So intent were they on their stories, not one of them lifted their eyes at her entrance.

Gabby moved quietly to the nursery door and twisted the handle. Nurse Jones sat in the rocking chair, mending in her lap. Sophia lay asleep on the bed.

Gabby sighed. She had missed her chance.

Nurse Jones looked up. "I'm sorry, miss. She was just too tired to wait."

Gabby nodded. "I understand." But she didn't. Not really. Why did no one come and fetch her? She would have abandoned her reading for Sophia. "I will check back in a while. Perhaps I can play a game with her once she awakens."

Nurse Jones just nodded and returned to her mending.

Gabby trudged through the school room, disappointed when Winston and Katie still did not acknowledge her presence. Miss Carter, however, looked up and scowled. Why must she be the only one to notice her presence?

Gabby stopped and turned back. "Winston, would you and Katie please go to your rooms for a moment? I need a word with Miss Carter."

Winston nodded, but Katie looked wide eyed at Miss Carter and then at Gabby. She nodded and they both disappeared into their rooms, closing the doors behind them.

"You have no right to dismiss my students." Miss Carter pushed herself to standing, her hands clenched at her side.

"And you have no right to scowl at me as you do. What have I done to earn your ire?" Gabby folded her arms across her chest, mostly to hide the shake in her hands. But if it added a sense of confidence, she would accept the help.

The lady scoffed. "As if you do not know."

Gabby stared, perplexed. How was she to know what the governess was thinking? "I have some ideas, but I do not know for certain."

"You come here with your accent and your large dowry, dangling them in front of our eligible gentlemen. While *English* ladies, those without such substantial means, are forced to seek employment. What gentleman would desire the likes of me—with no dowry—when they could have *you and your money*." She spat out the last words.

"I have no money of my own. Besides, what would you have me do? Spurn all gentlemen and lead them in your direction? Zis was not my doing. And if you zink my accent has been anyzing but a source of contempt for all who hear it, you are mistaken."

"I am to pity you, then? I am afraid you will be disappointed." The governess leaned and straightened the books on the bench.

"There is nothing to be done, then? Nothing I can do to change your opinion of me?"

The governess looked blankly at her. "Nothing comes to mind."

Gabby nodded. "Very well." Why had she thought to even try? She seemed destined to be disliked wherever she went. This did not bode well for the upcoming Season. She slipped out of the nursery room door.

Perhaps she could return to her rooms and work on a stitchery. Her shoulders slumped. A person could only stitch for so long before their eyes crossed and the colors ran together.

Gabby stopped in the middle of the corridor. What was she to do? None of her books held any appeal and her stitchery even less.

She twitched her lips to the side in thought. Had not Aline told her this house had a very grand library? The servants seemed to think it so. Maybe she could find something new to read?

Gabby padded down the stairs to the first floor. Aline had asked the servants below stairs where the library was, and she had passed the directions on to Gabby.

She had been leery to seek it out earlier—afraid she may encounter Lord Brinton. Was the library considered a private room? She had not considered them on friendly enough terms to venture down. But now, she may just be desperate enough to risk it.

Besides, Lord Brinton had told Lord Kirtley he was welcome to use it. Did that invitation not include her also? Her lips puckered. Probably not in the mind of Lord Brinton. But he had not expressly forbidden her from using it, either.

She turned down the corridor and counted the doors until she reached the one Aline had identified.

She placed her hand on the knob but pulled back without opening the door. What if this was not the right room? What if it was Lord Brinton's study or another private room?

She lifted her hand and knocked. Turning her head, she placed her ear close to the door but heard nothing. Gathering her courage, she twisted the knob and slowly pushed the door open. Peeking her head inside, relief flooded her. Not only *was* it the library, but it was empty.

Slipping inside, she turned in a circle, amazed at the vastness of it. The servants had not overstated its grandness.

Her father had possessed many books, but his three small bookcases were nothing compared to this two-story room with shelves lining every wall on both floors. Gabby moved to the center and looked at the upper floor. A door in nearly the same location as the one she had entered stood on the next level. Was it possible she could enter this room without the risk of seeing anyone on the stairs?

She spotted the narrow circular staircase in the far corner of the room. Lifting her skirts, Gabby hurried over and scurried up to the next floor. She went straight to the door to test it. Knowing her luck, it was locked, and she would just have to stare at it as it mocked her.

But when the knob twisted in her grip, she let out a little squeak of delight. Peering down the corridor, she found her bearings so she might use the upstairs door the next time she visited. Once she was sure she knew which door it was from the other side, she closed it and turned her attention to the shelves. There were shelves upon shelves of books. It was a pity they were all in English. She would love to read a book in her native language, though Lady Kirtley would likely frown upon her doing so. She insisted Gabby would never learn English better if she continued to read the French books—her father's books—she'd brought with her.

She pulled a few books off the nearest shelf and thumbed through them. Nothing caught her eye. Surely, in a library this vast, she could find something of interest.

The door beneath her clicked open and Gabby froze in place. Who was down there?

"Gabrielle? Are you in here?" Lady Kirtley's voice carried up from the lower level.

For a moment Gabby froze. If she did not answer, would the lady leave her alone? Gabby shook her head. No, she was looking for her. Lady Kirtley would keep at it until she discovered Gabby's whereabouts.

"I'm up here, Lady Kirtley."

The lady sighed. She was obviously frustrated if Gabby could hear it on the next level.

"Would you mind coming down? I would like to speak with you."

Gabby sagged and re-shelved the book she still held in her hand. Her mind flashed over everything that had happened in the last few days. Was there something she had done wrong? She could not think of anything—at least nothing Lady Kirtley had seen—but the irritation in the lady's voice indicated Gabby *had* done something.

Gabby walked down the spiral staircase, its charm suddenly dimming.

Lady Kirtley motioned to the couch by the fire.

Gabby sat down. "Have I done somesing wrong, my lady?"

"Well, that, for one." Lady Kirtley's shoulders dropped from their normally straight position.

Gabby stared at her. What was she talking about? "I'm sorry, my lady, but I do not know your meaning."

Lady Kirtley shook her head. "I am referring to you addressing me as my lady. We are in private. Have I not asked you to call me Eleanor repeatedly?" She shook her head. "When Peter arrived at Dovehaven with you, my first thought was that I was to have a sister, at long last. I love Peter, but I had always wished for a sister."

Gabby stared at Eleanor. She had wanted a sister? But why had she never treated Gabby as a sister? She paused. Or had she? It was not as if Gabby had a sister and knew how to interact with one.

"But when he left you with us, you seemed happier in the

schoolroom with the children and I assumed—rather uncomfortably —the role of mother. But now..." She stared down at her hands folded primly in her lap. "I find I don't want to be your mother, Gabrielle."

Did this mean Lady Kirtley was rethinking her offer to sponsor Gabby?

"I would prefer to be your sister, or at the very least, your friend."

Gabby's mouth dropped open. "My sister?"

Eleanor nodded and twisted the tip of her pinkie, a trait she had instilled in Gabby, until it was white. "I understand if that is too much. But could we at least try for friendship?" She breathed in deeply through her nose. "I will try not to lecture you or correct you so much. And maybe you could try calling me Eleanor, at least in private."

They were only to be as sisters in private? What did that mean they were when out in society?

"If we are sisters, I do not know why you should not call me Eleanor all of the time. But I understand if you are ill at ease with that notion."

Gabby smiled, her ramrod straight posture relaxing slightly. "If we are to be sisters, you should call me Gabby."

Eleanor sighed. Her shoulders assumed a similar stance to Gabby's, which to Gabby's relief looked very different from the sagging she'd seen moments ago. "I should like that, *Gabby*."

Eleanor looked around the room. "This is impressive. I had thought Dovehaven grand, but it is nothing to this place."

"Dovehaven is quite comparable to the rest of the house, but I am afraid I must give the library to Ivydale." She glanced over to Eleanor, wondering if their newfound sisterhood was about to be tested.

"You are being kind about the rest of the house, but you are certainly correct about this room." She eyed Gabby, a soft half smile on her lips. "Now that you have found it, will I ever see you again?"

Gabby chuckled. She liked this Eleanor very much. And she found the prospect of having a sister, or at the very least a friend, comforting. Would it keep some of the loneliness at bay? "At least you will know where to find me."

They sat in silence for a moment. Was their relationship the initial reason Eleanor had sought Gabby out? Or had it merely been brought on by Gabby addressing her as *my lady*?

"Was there something else you wished to discuss with me, *Eleanor*?" Gabby liked the thought of this closer connection to Eleanor, but it would take time to grow accustomed to it.

"Oh, yes." She placed a hand on Gabby's arm. "I wanted to inform you Lord Brinton has planned a lovely Christmas supper for five. I think you should wear the gold dress we bought before leaving London."

"But—"

Eleanor held up her hand. "I realize it is more elaborate than such an early supper—and a country one at that— requires, however, I think with it being Christmas, we can justify it. If you wear it with your red wrap, you will look stunning." Her eyes sparkled with excitement.

While Gabby had little notion of what it was to interact with a sister, this exact conversation was what she had imagined.

Gabby shrugged. "Why does it matter? I need not put on airs. Zere are no suitors for me at Ivydale."

Eleanor raised her brows, the corners of her mouth rising also. "We shall see about that."

Gabby folded her arms across her chest. "And what shall we see?"

"Come now, Gabby. Surely even you can see that Lord Brinton has taken an interest in you."

Gabby barked out a laugh. "What a good joke. Zat man detests all zings French. Especially me."

Eleanor waved away the protest. "Perhaps in the beginning, but that is not the case now. Even Hugh has noticed."

Gabby bit her lower lip, unsure what to think. The way her stomach twisted made her think she wanted Eleanor's words to be true. But why? Had she not seen repeatedly the mean, unyielding part of Lord Brinton's temperament? How could she desire such a man's affections? *If* he felt anything, which Gabby seriously doubted. "Any attentions he has shown toward me have only been a way for him to get away from Lady Brinton. Zere is no partiality, I assure you." She flipped open the book she found on the side table and looked up. "I've never been more certain about somezing in my life."

Eleanor shrugged, but the knowing spark in her eyes remained. "We shall see." She rose and quit the room, leaving Gabby alone with the books and heavy scent of leather.

Gabby stood, returning the book in her hands on the side table. She moved to the shelves, running her fingers over the spines, loving the feel of the cool leather and the indentions of the letters against her skin. What would it be like to have this many books at her fingertips anytime she wished to read them?

The door opened, and Gabby smiled. What had Eleanor forgotten? Had she thought of more reasons Lord Brinton had formed an attachment to her? "Did you forget to tell me somezing earlier?"

"Not that I recall. Did you think of something we needed to discuss?"

Gabby's finger froze on a book about hunting at the sound of Lord Brinton's gravelly voice.

She turned around slowly, clasping her hands behind her back. Would he be angry she was in here? He had not told her specifically she could come into the library.

"No. I did not zink of anything." She pulled her lip between her teeth.

Did Lady Kirtley truly believe there was interest on his part? It seemed unlikely—impossible, even. And yet, now that the notion had taken seed in her brain, Gabby couldn't help but think on it.

"I wondered if I might find you here. Kirtley indicated you are fond of reading." He rocked back on his heels, his eyes traveling around the room and then resting on her. He did not smile—not that she expected him to. She had invaded his space and he was angry.

"Yes. Here I am." She clutched the book to her chest, even

though she wasn't particularly interested in it. "I am sorry. Ees zis a private room? My abigail asked below stairs and zee servants did not mention zis room was private." She hated how thick her accent sounded. Usually, she liked to see him react to it. But not this time. Seeing him cringe and glower would wound her now; she blamed Eleanor and her misguided beliefs for the change. "My apologies."

Gabby looked up at him, bracing herself for what she was certain would be there. But he did not cringe nor scowl. Indeed, he seemed not to notice her accent as much as he had when she first arrived. Perhaps Eleanor's words held an element of truth. While Gabby still did not believe Lord Brinton had developed any sort of feeling for her, she could admit that his dislike of her had lessened. She found she liked that notion very much.

He shook his head. "No need to apologize. You may come to the library whenever you wish." Though his words were kind, his tone was still clipped; it was not the most welcoming invitation she had ever received. But if it meant she could look for books, she would accept it as it was.

Gabby put the book back on the side table. "You were likely seeking solitude just now. I will leave you alone." She turned toward the door, sadness clutching at her chest. She had not had enough time to find anything to read, and now she was being forced out. How long would he stay before she could return? Could she sneak in the upstairs door without him hearing and find a book? She bit down on her lip again.

His voice stopped her. "You do not have a book. Did you not find one to pique your interest?"

"Not particularly. But I have only just begun looking. I can return later when you are not here." She cringed. She had not meant it the way it sounded.

He shrugged. "You were here first. I did not intend to drive you out." He looked around the room. "Perhaps I can help you find something? What are you interested in reading? The gothic novels—I understand that is what young ladies like to read—are on the shelves nearest the fireplace."

She grunted. "Your information is wrong. Not all ladies prefer novels."

One eye squinted, but his lip curved ever so slightly. "I beg your pardon. I should have realized you are not like other ladies. What is it *you* are interested in?" Had his voice always had that silky tone to it?

"I like many zings. Historicals, poetry, essays." She raised her chin as his brows rose higher.

"There are some books that might interest you upstairs." He moved to the circular staircase, pausing with one foot on the step. "Are you coming?"

Gabby nodded and hurried to the staircase, following him up to the second floor. He moved with ease to the other side of the room. "They are right over there. If you'll let me show you."

She nodded and followed him around the perimeter of the room until they were almost opposite from the staircase. He bent slightly at the waist and pulled out a book, handing it over to her.

Gold letters etched deep into the leather. Gabby's breath hitched. *Candide, ou l'Optimisme.* Opening the book, she flipped through the pages and looked up at him. "Zis is in French."

He nodded. "Yes. All of these books are." He waved his hand in front of four shelves. There had to be close to a hundred books. Were all of them written in French?

She ran her finger over the title. This was one of the books her father had kept in his library, but she'd left it behind most grudgingly.

"You are welcome to take them to your room if you wish. Just please return them to the same location when you are finished." He smiled at her—genuinely smiled—and she could see why Lady Brinton acted as she did around him. Gabby had always thought him handsome, but this was different. This look made her stomach feel warm and tingly.

Gabby nodded. "Yes, of course. Zank you very much." She placed the book on the shelf and looked at the first row.

"And now, it is I who will leave you alone." One corner of his mouth quirked.

Gabby shook her head. "No. Zis is your library. I will return later to see what I can find." She smiled up at him. "Zank you for showing me."

He put a hand out, resting it on her arm. "Perhaps we can both enjoy the room together? I promise to be quiet."

She grinned. Who was this gentleman? "I promise to stay quiet as well." She looked down at his hand, still on her arm. He must have thought she objected to it because he pulled it back and cleared his throat. "My book is down below. I will leave you to explore."

Gabby watched him until the last wave of light brown hair disappeared below the stairs. She waited a moment longer for the flutters in her stomach to dissipate before she turned back toward the shelves. Something had changed just then, but she was not entirely certain what it meant.

Needing a distraction, Gabby ran her hand along the spines of the books sitting waist-high. What was a man, especially one with such a dislike for all things French, doing with so many books written in the language? Was he even able to read the books? Gabby could not imagine Lord Brinton spoke her native language. It seemed odd.

Unless his dislike had nothing to do with France. She frowned. Was it not the accent he did not like hearing, but rather just her voice? She had not considered the possibility before.

She thought back to that day at the Frost Fair. Had he not smiled at her until she spoke to him? That was when his nose had turned up and he'd said, "You're French." She could hear his voice as if he were standing next to her saying it even now. No, it *was* French that he did not like. So why did he have so many books written in the language? Gabby shrugged. She had promised him she would be quiet, but she *would* ask him about it. Someday.

CHAPTER 9

Aaron rested his elbow against the mantel in the drawing room, a glass of brandy in his hand. When he'd returned from church, instead of enjoying a fire, a glass of brandy, and a good book, he'd written letters and tried to figure out what to do about Lady Brinton.

Today's spectacle at the church had nearly brought him to his breaking point. He'd nearly hauled her into his office and had it out with her. Then he'd remembered his brother, and that had helped to stifle his anger. But the whole incident had made him realize that he needed to find a solution to her problems immediately because her problems were fast becoming his.

Henry. What would he think of this whole situation? He certainly would not appreciate Aaron ringing a peal over Rebekah, but Aaron did not know what else to do. His repeated spurns did not have the desired effect. If anything, her advances were increasing.

Aaron ran a hand through his hair. He was just so exasperated with her.

Perhaps he would not be so frustrated if it made any sense. While Aaron had not been in England when Henry and Rebekah had married, from Henry's letters Aaron had assumed it was a love match. He stroked at his chin. Rebekah did not play the part of a mourning widow, constantly flirting with Aaron. It made him think the love might have been on Henry's part alone.

And what was Rebekah thinking trying to secure a match with Aaron? 'Pon rep, her father was a vicar. Surely, he would not approve of a match between them. Gah. The more he thought on it, the more frustrated be became.

A deep breath passed through his lips. And then there was Miss Babineaux. His feelings for her had...well, he was not sure what they had done. They had changed, but he wasn't sure if it was simply because he did not have the energy to wage a battle on two fronts. The battle with Rebekah seemed the more important one. What was the saying? The enemy of my enemy is my friend?

He stared into his glass and swirled the liquid around. That saying did not fit his situation. Rebekah was not his enemy, she was only scared and confused. And Miss Babineaux? She was not his enemy either. Not anymore, at least. He could not think on her in that way, not since he'd seen her rocking Kirtley's little girl. It was too intimate of a moment for him to forget. He'd seen genuine love in her eyes when she had looked on the child.

The door opened. The footman showed Kirtley and his wife into the room. "Good evening, Brinton."

Aaron sketched a bow. "Lord and Lady Kirtley. Merry Christmas."

Lady Kirtley smiled and curtsied. "And to you, my lord."

The door opened a second time and Aaron lifted his gaze.

Miss Babineaux entered and for a moment he forgot to breathe.

Kirtley nudged him, and Aaron's breath whooshed out.

Aaron glanced over at his friend. Kirtley was grinning like an idiot. "I know that feeling, my friend." He nudged Aaron. "I experienced it when first I saw my Eleanor. If you are lucky, it will never cease, even after years of marriage."

Aaron looked over at Kirtley, knowing what the man said was

true. At least as it pertained to Lady Kirtley and Hugh. Aaron had noticed from nearly the first night of their visit that the earl was in love.

Aaron returned his attention back to Miss Babineaux who had come to stand next to Lady Kirtley. She wore a golden gown and a red wrap. Her already lovely eyes were now captivating, the dress bringing out the golden flecks in their deep, coffee color.

Aaron smiled. "Merry Christmas, Miss Babineaux." He knew he was staring but was at a loss as to how to pull his eyes away from her.

She dipped a curtsy. "*Joyeux Noël*, my lord."

He tilted his head to the side. Never had Merry Christmas sounded so pleasant to his ears.

Kirtley clapped Aaron on the back, laughter in his voice. "Thank you again, Brinton, for allowing us to invade your home over Christmastide. I am in your debt."

Aaron finally managed to pull his eyes away from Miss Babineaux. "I am pleased to have you. I think our holidays much livelier with your family here." He flicked a glance at Miss Babineaux. She had moved over and was speaking quietly with Lady Kirtley.

"Yes, I can see my family is what you are enjoying." Kirtley nudged Aaron again. The man was growing rather insufferable with all the nudging.

Aaron looked at him. "What? Are you inferring I do not wish you here? Because I can assure you that is not the case."

His mother and Lady Brinton entered before Kirtley could offer a reply. But from the look on Kirtley's face, Aaron supposed he would rather the interruption.

"I've never been happier in my life to have company," Aaron muttered. The thoughts of spending these holidays with only his mother to help him with Rebekah nearly made him break out in a sweat.

Kirtley chuckled.

Rebekah glanced up at the ceiling as she came toward him, and

Aaron remembered the kissing ball he'd fastened to the chandelier. He took a step to the side.

Rebekah frowned.

He leaned in slightly, dropping his voice to a whisper. "Lady Brinton. I have made some inquiries as to your situation." He clasped his hands behind his back. "I wanted you to know I had not forgotten about our discussion. I will inform you as soon as I have a response." He pulled out his pocket watch. Was it too much to hope for an early dinner? He kept a discreet eye on Rebekah. She'd proven she would do whatever it took to get what she wanted.

A light touch landed on his arm and Aaron jerked.

Miss Babineaux stepped back. "Pardon."

"Please excuse me. I was woolgathering and did not hear your approach."

She took a tentative step forward. "I wished only to sank you for allowing me zee use of your books. I am enjoying zem very much."

He smiled, his eyes crinkling ever so slightly. It was the first real smile he'd given in...he twisted his head to the side. Well, he did not remember how long it had been. "I'm glad someone is reading them again. I have not looked at them in years."

Her brow creased. "You speak French, my lord?"

"Oui." He grinned when her brow raised in surprise. "*Comment allez-vous ce soir*?" When her eyes widened, he threw his head back and laughed, drawing the attention of all in the room.

Miss Babineaux lowered her voice. "When did you learn French? When you were in the army?"

Aaron shook his head. "No. My brother Henry and I had a French tutor until we left for Eton."

Her brow furrowed again. "Zen why—" She pulled her bottom lip between her teeth and shook her head. "Zank you again for letting me borrow them."

"You are most welcome." Aaron looked down at her. Emotions swam across her face faster than he could identify them.

He knew the question she had been going to ask.

He should tell her. She had the right to know. But it was Christmas day, and it didn't feel like the right time. Tonight was a time to feast and sing carols. Not remember pains from the past.

A hand warmed his arm, and he smiled down at Miss Babineaux. But his smile faded when he looked into the face of his sister-in-law. How had Miss Babineaux abandoned him so quietly? More importantly, why was Rebekah doing this? There were so many things about Henry they could share if she would not be so intent on developing a relationship with Aaron. Friendship was all Aaron could ever offer her.

"Dinner is served, my lord."

"Thank you, Collins."

The butler bowed and turned from the room.

His mother took the arm of Lord Kirtley. Aaron smiled. "Mother, it's Christmas. May we dispense with the formalities tonight?" He looked to Kirtley. "I am sure Kirtley would not object to it."

Kirtley shook his head. "Not at all, Brinton."

Aaron held his arm out to the dowager viscountess. "Mother, may I escort you in to dinner?"

She scoffed but put her hand on his arm. "Henry would never have dispensed with formalities just because it is Christmas."

Aaron pulled his mother to the side. He had abided the mentions of Henry long enough. "Lady Brinton, could you please show our guests to the dining room? Mother and I need a word."

"Aaron." His mother pulled on his arm. "Surely this can wait. You are showing very poor manners."

"I am certain I am, Mother. But this cannot wait." He paused as everyone vacated the room then turned to face her, his arms crossed over his chest.

"What is the meaning of this, Aaron? You are acting abominably. Henry would never be so rude."

Aaron sucked in a breath. "That is what we need to discuss."

She looked at him as if he were daft. "What? I have no notion what you are speaking of."

"I am not Henry, Mother. No matter how often you remind me of that fact, I will never be Henry. I am sorry he died. I am sorry he is not here to do everything just as you like. But *he is not here*. I, however, am. And I am not going anywhere." His head twitched to the side. "Please, stop comparing me to him. I know I will never be the man he was. But I am doing my best."

His mother's mouth hung open, looking very much like the fish that would undoubtedly be served for dinner. She swallowed once... then twice before snapping her mouth shut. "I know you are not Henry. Why would you ever think I thought you less than your brother?"

Now it was Aaron whose mouth hung open. How could she not know? Did she not hear herself speak? "You have not spoken to me once since my return without using the phrase *if Henry were here*."

His mother's brow puckered.

"If Henry were here, we would not dispense with formalities." Aaron spoke in a high-pitched tone, mimicking his mother's voice. "If Henry were here, he would not leave London until after Lord Trenton's ball. If Henry—"

"Yes, I get the idea." His mother looked down at her hands. "I had not thought of how you would interpret my words. I was only..." She stopped. "No. You are right. I was comparing you." She paused, as if trying to formulate her words. Her head shook back and forth. "There are few similarities between you and your brother. I should not have tried to make you like him. I had just never envisioned you as Lord Brinton, and I suppose it's been difficult accepting it."

It stung to hear her confirm his belief. "I never envisioned it either, Mother. But here we are and there is nothing either of us can do about it."

She placed a hand on his arm. "I did not intend to agree that you are less than your brother, Aaron. You have many qualities that will make you a better viscount than Henry ever could have been. You are firm and decisive. And I believe you have a far better head for management. But you are also oft time unyielding and almost tyrannical."

Aaron smiled at the title he had come to call his own.

She continued, oblivious to his smile. "You have been away for so long, sometimes I feel I do not even know you anymore." She sighed. "And I am still mourning your brother."

Aaron felt as though she had plunged a knife into his gut. He hadn't taken into account her grief over losing Henry. What kind of son did not note his mother's suffering? Perhaps his mother did not grieve as others might, with bouts of tears, but as he looked back, he could see her pain when she mentioned Henry's name.

He placed his hand over hers. "Perhaps we both need to change our thinking and accept each other for who we are, not for what we think the other *should* be."

Her eyes glossed over with unshed tears.

Aaron did not remember ever seeing his mother cry. The thought that she cried now, because of him, nearly brought him to tears as well.

His mother placed a hand on his face. "You *are* very much like your father, though."

Aaron's Adam's apple bobbed. He had always thought Henry most like his father. "Oh? How so?"

She smiled. "He was also hard and unyielding. But like him, there are times, as rare as they are, when your softer side shows." She patted his cheek, her head dropped to one side. "Just make certain you do not scare a certain young lady off before she has a chance to see that softer side. I know of your kindness, but not everyone does."

"I do not feel that way for Reb—"

She held up her hand. "I was not speaking of Rebekah." Her face clouded over. "I'm not certain what she is thinking, presenting herself as a light-skirt. If Henry were here—"

"If Henry were here, she would not need to flirt with me, now would she?" While Aaron was frustrated with Rebekah, he still found if difficult to hear his mother speak ill of her. The dowager likely did not know of the uncertainly the current Lady Brinton felt.

His mother shrugged, a smile playing around her lips. "I suppose that's true."

He sucked in a deep breath. For the first time since his return, his shoulders felt lighter, even as his heart pounded over his mother's reference to "a certain young lady." She could only be speaking of Miss Babineaux. "Come, Mother. Let us join our guests for dinner."

Everyone was chatting amiably when Aaron and his mother walked into the dining room. He was grateful to see that somehow Rebekah was seated at the other end of the table, putting distance between them.

He looked at everyone's smiling faces. Even Rebekah seemed to be happy. This was the moment he wanted to remember in years to come. This was what Christmas should be.

Aaron and his mother settled in and a line of footmen, each carrying a platter, lined up at his mother's side.

"In honor of our French guest, I thought it entertaining to dine *à la française*," his mother said in a remarkably poor accent.

Aaron looked to Miss Babineaux seated next to him.

Her eyes danced with amusement. "You are too kind, my lady. Thank you."

Aaron cleared his throat. "It appears I am not the only one wishing to dispense with formalities this evening." Dining in the French style, with everyone dishing their own food, was not the custom at his mother's parties. She usually preferred the more formal *à la russe*, where the servants would serve the guests each dish.

Aaron winked at his mother; proud she had embraced this less formal style. Especially considering she had done so even before their talk. This kind of service would have to have been planned.

She shrugged, describing each dish as a footman set it on the table.

Aaron looked at the platters filled with food. How were they to eat even a quarter of all this food? His thought flitted for a moment to his men still serving in France. Were they eating this well? He knew the truth and his spirits sagged. Closing his eyes, he pushed the melancholy to the side. Today he could do nothing about his men and their hunger. That was something for him to deal with in Lords. For now, he would enjoy the company and the food. His men would want that for him.

He reached for the tureen of onion soup, ladling out an ample portion. He winced when he looked at how much he had taken. It was not as if he were starving on the battlefield. He sighed. It was not as if he could put it back.

Aaron looked to Kirtley. "Would you prefer the onion or the hare soup?"

"The onion smells delicious. But who says I have to settle for just one?" Kirtley's bowl held nearly as much soup as Aaron's. He devoured it and looked for the hare.

Aaron grinned, thankful his friend was here.

"Aaron, would you pass the onion soup?" Rebekah's voice was softer than he'd heard it in days. She smiled at him, and he relaxed when he saw there was no flirting involved. A footman approached, and Aaron handed him the tureen to deliver to the other end of the table.

Aaron nodded to her. This was the Rebekah Henry had described to him. Quiet and reserved, but sweet. Where had this girl been for the last four days?

He retrieved the fish platter and dished it for himself and Miss Babineaux.

The meal was more than filling and Aaron did not remember ever having roast goose taste so good. And it had been an age since he'd had Yorkshire pudding. He leaned back in his seat and ran a hand over his full belly.

Aaron watched, listening and observing his family and friends. Miss Babineaux smiled often—something Aaron was becoming rather fond of—speaking and laughing with Lady Kirtley multiple times throughout the meal. Rebekah was quiet but still contributed to the conversation.

This was the best Christmas he'd had in recent memory.

A moan sounded from his throat as the footmen placed macaroons, gingerbread cake and Shrewsbury cake on the table. "Ah, I am done for; I do not believe I can eat another bite."

"Come, Aaron. It is Christmas. You must at least take a bite of each." His mother watched him until he had dished himself some of each.

"Mother, how are you to eat dessert if you are watching me?"

She put some gingerbread on her plate and sighed deeply.

He chuckled, knowing she was just as full as he was.

"Perhaps we can have dessert removed to the drawing room. I know I will better enjoy it if I am not so full as now." Aaron pushed back from the table. "I don't know about you Kirtley, but I have no desire to speak of politics nor do I have room for even one glass of port. What do you say to skipping all that and joining the ladies for some carols?" Aaron stood, straightening to his full height and discreetly stretching.

Kirtley stood and offered his arm to the dowager and Lady Brinton. "I do love carols. What of you, Lady Brinton?"

Aaron did not hear her response as Kirtley led her from the room.

He offered his arm to Lady Kirtley and Miss Babineaux. "Tell me, my lady. Does Miss Babineaux sing half as prettily as she hums?"

Miss Babineaux's cheeks turned a shade rosier.

"I don't recall ever hearing Gabrielle hum. But I have heard her sing. And it is lovely. Sophia sleeps best when Gabrielle sings her a lullaby. She will be quite the performer at the musicales this Season."

Gabrielle? That was her Christian name? Had he heard it at their introduction and forgotten? It was likely. He grimaced as he remembered his behavior toward her—both times they had met. The tips of his ears burned. If Gabrielle had not reminded him of Mireille, would things have been different?

It was doubtful. As much as he hated to admit it, it was not just her voice that had put him at odds with Gabrielle. It was her nationality. Over the last five years, he'd allowed himself to hate an entire nation. How had that happened?

They stepped inside the drawing room. His mother, Kirtley, and Rebekah were already seated in chairs next to the fire, the yule log hanging over the grate on both sides. This log may not last all the way to Epiphany, but there were several others cut from the same tree to replace this one once it burned down.

The pianoforte sat against the opposite wall.

The hands on his arm dropped away. Lady Kirtley moved to sit beside her husband, and Gabrielle—now that he knew her name, he had a hard time thinking of her as Miss Babineaux— stepped away from him.

"Are we ready to sing?" He looked to Gabrielle. Hers was the voice he was most eager to hear. He remembered her in the nursery, the youngest of Kirtley's children on her lap, but if she had been singing, it was quiet, and he had not heard it.

His mother nodded. "Yes, but I should like to play a game of snapdragons before the evening is over."

Rebekah pushed off the couch. "I can play the pianoforte, but I would prefer not to sing."

Aaron's mother patted her arm. "Yes. Let us not have a repeat of the Millers' musicale."

Rebekah pinked and Aaron scowled at his mother.

"Do not look at me so, Aaron. Some are born to play and others to sing. Our dear Rebekah is quite accomplished on the pianoforte. But it does not follow that she can sing."

While he knew his mother did not mean to offend poor Rebekah, with every word she spoke, Rebekah's cheeks grew ruddier.

Aaron held up his hand. "Thank you, Rebekah, for playing." He and his mother had resolved many issues this evening. Perhaps he could wait for another day to broach the subject of Rebekah's singing —or rather his mother's opinion of it.

Everyone gathered around the piano and Rebekah looked around at the group. "What shall you sing first?"

Lady Kirtley spoke up. "Do you know *God Rest Ye Merry, Gentlemen*? It was a favorite when I was a child."

Rebekah played the first notes and then nodded her head when it was time for them to join in.

His mother was correct; Rebekah was a proficient on the instrument. It was like a completely different woman sat at the pianoforte than the one he'd seen the last few days. She exuded a quiet confidence with her hands on the keys.

Everyone sang with feeling, the spirit of the holiday evident. Kirtley—as Aaron had discovered at Eton—still could not sing a note, but that did not quell his enthusiasm.

When the song finished, Aaron turned to Miss Babineaux. "I am surprised you knew that song so well. I thought it was an English carol."

"It is. Peter lived with us for two Christmastide seasons. He taught my father and me all the songs he could remember. Before he left, I made him tell me the words of each song and I wrote them down. Every year my father and I would sing those songs, along with our traditional French songs."

Aaron smiled, attributing his over abundant joy to the Christmas season. "Is there a French song you would like to sing, Miss Babineaux?"

"Do you know *Un Flambeau, Jeannette, Isabelle?*" She looked at Rebekah, who shook her head. Gabrielle motioned to the seat at the pianoforte.

Rebekah moved to the side and allowed Gabrielle to take the seat. Gabrielle placed her hands on the keyboard and her fingers flowed across each key, the music floating out of the instrument. It was quite lovely. But then she started to sing.... Aaron was captivated. He had never heard anything like it.

Un flambeau, Jeannette, Isabelle—
Un flambeau! Courons au berceau!

Her voice was even more beautiful than Lady Kirtley had implied. If angels were singing, Aaron felt confident Gabrielle would be among them.

As she started the second verse, a memory niggled in his brain. He had heard this song before. He hummed along at first, not remembering all the words, but by the end, he sang along with her. Their voices blended, although her voice made his sound better, rather than the opposite.

She glanced up quickly from the keys, a smile on her face. Then she continued with the third and fourth verse, the two of them singing a duet.

When the song was over, she pulled her fingers off the keys—the piano still vibrating— and relinquished the stool to Rebekah.

Rebekah waved Gabrielle back. "But you play so well. Why do you not play another?" Was there a hint of a challenge in her voice, or was it resentment?

Gabrielle shook her head. "I am only able to play a few songs. Please, you play much better than I do. I've had my moment to remember. Now it is your turn."

Rebekah narrowed her eyes slightly but returned to the seat. "Do you know this one?" She played the first few strains of *While Shepherds Watched Their Flocks* and they all joined in. They followed that with the *First Nowell.*

Aaron watched Gabrielle as she sang each song. Several were new to her, but still, she hummed along to the later verses. How had he ever thought she was anything like Mireille? Now that he really listened to her voice, it sounded nothing like that French menace.

But with one realization came another. It did not matter what he knew now. He could not take back those first few days and the terrible way he had treated her.

CHAPTER 10

Aaron paced in front of the fireplace in his study. He raked his hand through his hair and down the back of his neck. They had sung carols until everyone decided it was too late to play Snapdragon. Everyone agreed they would play the game this evening instead. From his view, the time had been better spent singing.

Aaron had gone to bed with thoughts of Gabrielle swirling in his head. What had changed from five days ago to today? How had his opinion of her shifted so dramatically? He'd gone from trying to avoid her and wishing her as far from his home as possible to her filling his dreams and his every waking moment.

Was it just her voice? Had he changed his opinion of her because she sang so prettily?

His brow furrowed.

A knock sounded at the door and Rebekah poked her head in. "My lord, I was hoping you could accompany me to the tenant cottages to deliver the St. Stephen's gifts."

Aaron stopped his pacing. "I see no reason why I could not. What time did you wish to go?"

She stepped fully into the room. "I hoped you would help me assemble the baskets first. Then we could deliver them."

Aaron shrugged. It would not answer the questions plaguing him, but it would allow him to postpone thinking on them for a time. "I am happy to help. Is my mother not available?"

Rebekah shook her head. "When I married your brother, she turned the task over to me. She said it was the duty of the current viscountess."

That sounded very much like something his mother would say. She never had liked the delivery of St. Stephan's Day gifts. "Then how may I be of assistance?"

Rebekah smiled widely and waved him toward the door. "Come with me. We set everything up in the west parlor."

Aaron eyed her wearily. Which Rebekah would deliver the baskets with him? Flirty or quiet? He very much hoped it was the latter. Quiet Rebekah was not much of a conversationalist, but she did not irritate him either.

They stepped out into the corridor and walked side by side to the parlor. The door was open, and a table sat on the far side. Baskets were piled up at one end, while baked goods and stacks of clothing filled the rest. There was gingerbread and crocks of soup from the night before. Large loaves of bread and biscuits filled many trays.

Aaron whistled. "I have not helped gather the presents together in many years. I may need a reminder of how to do this most efficiently."

Rebekah showed him what she wanted in each basket. They distributed the clothes and then moved on to the food. When they ran out of gingerbread, they switched it for biscuits, and then Shrewsbury cake.

Aaron was pleased to see that quiet, but efficient Rebekah had joined him. He imagined they could have developed a friendship, had she been this way from the beginning.

When the last basket was covered, he rotated his shoulders. "I will find a few footmen and have them put these on the sledge." He moved toward the bell pull in the corner when Rebekah called to him. He stopped and turned back. "Yes?"

She was at his side in moments, her hands on his chest. Before Aaron even knew what Rebekah was about, she went up on tiptoes and pressed her lips to his.

Aaron stepped back and stared at her. "What the blazes are you doing?"

She pointed to the kissing ball hanging above them.

"I don't care if there is a kissing ball. Your actions are improper."

She gawked at him. "What do you want me to do? I tried to be like the debutantes I saw in London, but that only seemed to push you further away. I tried to be quiet and reserved, but then you completely ignored me. What am I to do to get you to see me?"

Aaron's mouth hung open. "My brother has not yet been in the grave a year. You have not even completed your mourning period. Did you think this behavior would entice me to marry you? It is not possible, Rebekah. You are my sister in the eyes of God and the church. No clergyman would perform the marriage. Surely your father would not give his approval." Aaron shook his head. "Henry led me to believe yours was a marriage of love. But I can see, now, it was only on his part."

A squeaky sob sounded. Rebekah put a hand to her mouth and blinked twice, her eyes shining with tears. She let out another sob and turned, running from the room.

Aaron stood with his hands on his hips. He did not know if she was crying because of his rejection or his harsh words about her conduct. But either way, what he had spoken was just, and she had needed to hear it.

He looked at the table of baskets and sighed. Now what was he to do? It was doubtful his mother would willingly deliver these with him. He growled. It appeared he would be delivering the gifts on his own.

Why could Rebekah not have left well enough alone? It was not as if she was the first young woman left widowed. Others before her had survived, and without marrying their brother.

He walked the last steps to the pull and yanked several times, much harder than was necessary.

"Are you well, my lord?"

Gabrielle—Miss Babineaux. He really should quit thinking of her so informally—stood just outside the door, her hands clasped behind her back.

He nodded. "Yes. Lady Brinton and I were to deliver these baskets to the tenants, but she...has taken ill and cannot join me."

"That is terrible. I hope she will recover quickly."

He shrugged. "I do not believe it is serious."

"If there is anything I can do—"

Aaron stepped forward. "Actually—" He paused and shook his head. "Never you mind."

"Are you certain? I do not mind helping."

Aaron eyed her. Should he ask for her help? This was not something that was any of her concern, but the thought of delivering these gifts on his own was daunting. With Gabrielle at his side, however, it could be an enjoyable chore.

"Would you come with me to the cottages? I have not been home in more than five years. I do not even know what to say to my tenants."

Gabrielle pulled her bottom lip in. "I do not know these people and have never done such a thing. Would not your mother be better suited?"

"Yes, she would." He grunted. "But she will never be prevailed upon to go out in this weather." He glanced out the window. "I need to go. I believe it will start snowing again soon."

She played with her little finger. He had noticed she did it when she was thinking or was it when she was nervous? "If you need help, I will go with you."

His shoulders sagged. "Oh, thank you, Gabrielle."

She stared at him and it took him a moment to realize what he had done. Gah. Had he not just warned himself about thinking of her so informally?

"I'm sorry. I did not mean to be so presumptuous."

She smiled. "You need not apologize. I was only surprised." She looked like she wished to say more, but her eyes flicked to the window and she stopped. "I believe you are correct. Another storm is coming." She turned toward the door. "Allow me to change my clothes and I shall meet you in the entry."

Aaron thumped his forehead with his fist. She had not told him he could use her Christian name, but when he had, she hadn't told him *not* to do it again. He grumbled. Now he did not know what he should call her.

She had walked several paces when he reached out a hand to stop her. Electricity surged up his arm. "Thank you again," he said, his voice low.

She nodded. "You are welcome."

This time when she turned away, Aaron let her go.

A maid waited in the hall for Gabrielle to pass and stepped inside. "You rang, my lord?"

"Yes. I need Jacobs to ready the sledge. I also need several footmen to take these baskets out once the sledge is ready." He motioned to the window. "And we need to do it quickly. Another storm is coming."

The maid shook her head. "I'm sorry, my lord. But none of the footmen are here. Most of the servants are off today." She paused. "It is St. Stephens Day."

Aaron grumbled. How had he forgotten that the staff was off for the day? It was no wonder the house was so quiet.

"Very well; I will see to it myself."

She curtsied again. "I believe there is still a hand in the stable. I will ask him to ready the sledge."

Aaron sighed. "Thank you, Anne. And tell the stable hand thank you also."

She nodded and hurried from the room.

He made his way to his study, pulling several small pouches of coins out of his top drawer. It wouldn't make them rich, but hopefully, it would allow his tenants coal for the rest of the winter, or something else if they had a need.

He hurried to the entry to wait for Gabrielle.

He chided himself. As long as he thought of her by her Christian name rather than Miss Babineaux, he risked possibly offending her yet again.

Aaron fetched his greatcoat and beaver from the coatroom, grabbing Gabrielle's pelisse and bonnet. Thunder and turf! Now that he had started, he could not seem to stop thinking of her as Gabrielle. He stepped from the room and draped the coats over the back of a chair. Pulling on his greatcoat, he dropped the pouches of coins into his pockets. Then he worked his fingers into his gloves while he waited for Gabrielle. He shrugged. He truly was a nodcock.

"The sledge is ready, my lord." A red-nosed stable hand bowed while discreetly trying to rub warmth into his hands.

"I suppose that means you are waiting on me." Gabrielle, gah, Miss Babineaux stepped down onto the tile floor.

Aaron lifted her coat from the chair and helped her slip it on, then waited while she tied the ribbons of her bonnet.

He stepped up beside her. "On the positive side, the cold will not allow us much time for visiting."

She tilted her head. "Do you not wish to visit with your tenants? How will you develop a relationship with them if you do not take the time to know their needs?"

He shrugged, but a smile pulled at the corners of his mouth. "Is it not acceptable to develop a relationship in the springtime, when the weather is more amiable?" He opened the front doors and motioned her out.

A gust of wind blew into the house, pulling her bonnet ribbons taut. She gave him a half-smile. "Normally I am not one for procrastination, but perhaps today you are correct."

He chuckled. "Let's be on our way."

He handed her up onto the seat of the sledge. It was not a fancy sledge by any means, used mostly by Jacobs and the stable hands to move hay bales to and from the stable in conditions such as this. The current weather was rare here in Kent so they'd never had need of anything beyond the simple sledge.

Gabrielle sat on the bench with her back straight and her hands folded primly in her lap. Looking at her, he could see her mother's aristocracy in her air.

He swung up and took hold of the reins. The sledge had no sides or even rails to keep the baskets from tumbling off. Slow and easy was the course for today, even if the weather did not understand it as such. He clucked his tongue, and the horses set into motion.

They reached the first cottage, and Aaron helped Gabrielle down. She collected a basket from the back of the sledge and together they walked to the first door.

Aaron knocked, shifting from one foot to the other, trying to ward off the cold.

An older woman with gray streaked hair opened the door. She looked leerily at them.

Aaron smiled. "Good day, Mrs. Cole. And happy St. Stephen's Day. It has been a long time since last we meet. I hope you and your husband are well."

She nodded, but the weariness did not leave her eyes.

Aaron's breath hovered in front of his face. He looked to Gabrielle and nodded.

She thrust the gift forward.

"Here is a small token of appreciation." He removed a pouch from his coat pocket and placed it on top of the cloth covering the contents of the basket. "Please let myself or Mr. Bancock know if you have a need. We will do what we can to assist you."

She nodded. "Thank ye." She shut the door.

Gabrielle looked up at him with raised brows. "You were right. The cold is keeping conversation to a minimum."

He raised a shoulder. "It also helps that I have not seen these people in years. One or two of them are new since I left for the continent."

They moved on to the next cottage. The reception was similar, and they were on their way quickly.

At the third cottage, a young woman with a belly swollen with child opened the door. "Ah, Mrs. Perkins. Happy St. Stephen's Day to you. We have brought you a gift to show our appreciation for you."

The door opened wider, and a man appeared beside the woman. His leg was missing below the knee, a wooden peg in its place. "Major, is that you?"

Aaron smiled. "Good day, Perkins. How are you and yours?"

He nodded. "As well as can be expected." He rubbed at his knee. "You know 'ow it is. This cold brings out the old aches and pains."

Aaron rubbed at his shoulder. He'd not noticed the ache until now.

He looked to Gabrielle, and she handed over the basket. "This is for you." She smiled and placed the gift in his arms. "It is an honor to meet one of Aaron's friends."

Ah, she had called him Aaron. Surely, that implied she was amiable to him calling her Gabrielle.

Perkins's smile faded, and he squinted at Gabrielle then looked to Aaron.

It took a moment, but then Aaron's stomach dropped. He had not considered how Perkins and Millard would react if they heard Gabrielle speak. Seeing Perkins's face, he thought about it now. Had it not taken Aaron nearly a week, constantly in her presence, to see past her accent? He barely heard it now. But Perkins and Millard had not had the time Aaron had to find the good in Gabrielle.

He swallowed. This interaction could turn ugly rather quickly if Aaron did not get Gabrielle away.

He put his hand on the small of her back and moved it slowly to her waist. She flinched slightly but did not move out of his arm. He pulled her back several steps. "I shall not keep you out in the cold any longer, Perkins. When it warms, we must reminisce about the good times."

"Did you forget zee coins?" Gabrielle whispered into his shoulder.

"Ah, Perkins. I was so happy to see you, my old friend, I nearly forgot to give you this." Aaron quickly extracted a pouch of coins and tossed it to the man. "Hopefully, it will buy you some extra coal to keep those aches at bay."

Perkins glanced to Aaron's hand around Gabrielle and nodded slowly, one eye squinting nearly closed.

Aaron lifted his hand in a wave. Turning them both around, he headed for the sledge. "Perhaps you should not say anything to the tenants. Or better yet, why do you not remain with the sledge while I deliver the next basket?"

Her brow furrowed. "Did I say somesing wrong?"

Funny how he noticed her accent now. He shook his head. "No. It is my fault. I did not consider that Perkins and my next tenant, Mr. Millard, may not take kindly to you—being French."

Gabrielle pinched her lips together tightly. "Ah. You served with them in the war."

He nodded. It felt lacking, as if there was more he should say. But what? Now was not the time to tell her of Mireille.

She nodded. "If zat is what you wish."

His shoulders sagged. It was not what he wished. He quite enjoyed having her by his side, but he could not risk it. While he'd never thought of Perkins or Millard as dangerous men, he knew their hatred—similar to his—for Mireille. He feared the men may take that hatred out on Gabrielle. Had not Aaron done exactly that?

"Please, do not be sad. It is nothing you did. It is merely the circumstances." He looked up at the sky. "I will hurry with this one and then we can do the others together."

She nodded. "You need not apologize. I came to help. If staying with the sledge helps you, zat is what I will do. Zese are your tenants. Not mine."

How had he confused her for Mireille? Now he could see the stark contrast between the two women. He had let hatred color his previous views of Gabrielle.

He had the sudden urge to kiss her, but he jumped from the sledge instead. He did not think she would appreciate the gesture as much as he would.

He grabbed a basket from the back and hurried to the next cottage. Millard answered the door, the patch over his eye slightly askew.

"Major." Millard stuck his hand out for Aaron to shake. "It's good to see you, sir."

Aaron smiled. "And you, Millard. I will not keep you out in this cold long. But I wanted you to have this." He handed over the gift and dropped the coins on top.

"Thank ye, sir." He shifted. "I s'pose I should get used to calling you *my lord* from now on."

Aaron smiled. "Major will do, as well."

Millard's head bobbed. He glanced toward the sledge. "Who is the miss there?" He grinned. "You courtin' a lady, sir?"

Aaron chuckled. It was not the first time he'd thought about it. "No. She is a guest staying at Ivydale. Lady Brinton took ill and could not accompany me, so Miss—" Aaron paused. "The young lady agreed to accompany me instead."

Millard grinned. "She does pretty up the sledge, sir." He winked as if he knew something Aaron was keeping secret.

Aaron looked back. "Yes, she certainly does." His stomach fluttered.

He cleared his throat as if Millard knew about the flurry happening in his gut. "Yes, well. I should let you get back inside where it is warm." He clapped the man on the shoulder. "Stay warm, Lieutenant."

The man looked solemn. "I will, sir. After some of those nights in France, I don't believe I could ever be that cold again. At least now I have a roof over me head."

"I am grateful for that, as well. Good day, Mr. Millard."

Aaron climbed back into the sledge and took up the reins. "Again, I apologize for making you stay. You are probably freezing from sitting here."

She shrugged. "All will be well."

They rode in silence for a moment. "How long have those men been tenants here?"

Aaron sighed. "About two years."

"And it is your doing?" She looked at him in a way he had never seen before.

"After a particularly bad skirmish, both men received injuries that ensured the end of their military service." He gripped the reins tighter. "If you've been to London, you surely saw how well England takes care of her soldiers when they come home. Neither man would have been able to find work in their conditions. I gave them letters of introduction before they left and wrote to Henry. I promised to pay their leases until they could manage it themselves."

"You are very kind. Not many commanders would do as much for their men." She bit her lip. "I am surprised there were only two in those circumstances."

Aaron ran a hand through his hair. "There weren't. There were many." He kneaded his neck with one hand. "I secured jobs with my friends for as many of them as I could, but there were always more needing help. Soon, I had no more friends to prevail upon."

She placed her hand on his arm. "You did what you could. You need not feel guilty."

"Yes, well, perhaps my coming home to take over the family title does have its advantage. Now I can try to help from within Lords." He sounded more optimistic than he really was. Getting any kind of reform on the treatment of soldiers was an uphill battle. But that did not mean it was not a battle worth fighting.

CHAPTER 11

Gabby pulled her legs up and under her skirt, settling into the corner of the settee. The fire flamed high, warming everything around it.

She glanced out the window. Snow had been falling yet again since the afternoon before. She and Aaron had not made it back to the house before their shoulders and heads were covered with flakes.

Gabby wondered if they would ever make it back to Dovehaven. She hugged herself. Although lately she hadn't minded being snowed in at Ivydale. There were worse places to be in weather like this—places without gravely voices and eyes the color of the sky just before a storm raged the sea.

She sighed. She was just being silly. Aaron had given no indication he was partial to her. She was taking his new kindness and interpreting it as something it was not.

She returned her attentions to her book. Her *French* book. She felt slightly guilty for reading it in secret, knowing that Eleanor would likely disapprove. But the guilt was not strong enough to make Gabby stop. Did that make her immoral or even evil? Her parish priest growing up would surely have thought so.

She shook her head. It was not as if she was reading sinful books. She just did not agree with Eleanor's notion on the subject.

The library door opened, and Aaron entered, his attention on the book in his hand. He did not see her immediately, which gave her a moment to study him openly. His wavy, light brown hair was cut shorter than most gentlemen she had seen about London, and naturally flowed to one side around his face. Currently, a path of hair down the middle of his head stood on end. She smiled, knowing it was likely from him running his hand through it. What would it be like to be those fingers? Her face heated, even as she imagined the softness of his hair.

She exhaled quietly through her nose, not wanting to disturb him just yet. But she was not quiet enough. He looked up. His eyes sparkled and his lips parted slightly. She thought she detected a hint of a smile. Was it because he saw her or had something else put it there?

"I'm sorry, Gabrielle. I did not notice you there."

She waved away his apology. "It is your library, my lord. You need not apologize for visiting it."

He closed the book and dropped his hand to his side. "Nevertheless, I did not intend to disturb you. I will leave you to your reading." He turned to leave.

"You are not interrupting," she nearly shouted at him. "You may stay if you wish." What a dimwitted thing to say. He did not need her permission to remain in his own library. "Er, not that you need my permission. That is to say, it would not bother me if you stayed."

He raised a brow, his lips pursed, although not enough to hide the twitch. "Do you wish me to stay, Gabrielle?"

She shrugged, even as her muscles went weak. "Whatever you desire, my lord." Her face pinked. What had happened to her? She could not seem to get a coherent sentence out this morning. *Whatever you desire?* Some men would take such words as an invitation. But she believed she knew Aaron well enough to know he would not interpret her words in such a way. "We could talk if that is what you wish."

Zut, she sounded like a complete idiot.

He smiled and sat down on the other end of the couch. "And what would you wish to talk about?"

She lifted her shoulders. What had she done? Now he sat—much closer than Gabby had expected—waiting for her to come up with something they could talk about. Her mind went blank. She did not even know if she could think of something to say in French.

"Why do you not like me?"

That was what her brain came up with? Blank nothingness would have been better than discussing that.

He grinned. "Who told you that I dislike you?"

Was he trying to avoid the question? "I may have misspoken. Why *did* you hate me?" She should have let it go. He had given her the chance to change the subject, but ever since he had shown her the shelves of books in the library, she had wondered. How had a man, who had obviously once enjoyed French and perhaps even France, come to abhor it so? Was it just the war that had tainted his views?

The grin faded. "I would not say I *hated* you."

She snort-laughed and he raised an amused brow. "Abhor? Loathe? Which do you prefer? They all describe the looks on your face when I first arrived. Your nose even curled the first time we met. If that is not hate, I do not know what is."

He nodded slowly and placed his book on the side table and turned to face her. "Perhaps you are right." He paused. "It was a misguided *dislike*"—he grinned at his word choice—"based on a misconception."

"Because I was French? But you studied French, bought French books. How did you come to abhor an entire nation? Is that what war does?" As the words dripped from her lips, she felt naïve. And yet, she'd lived on the opposite side of that war and she did not dislike all Englishmen. How was it different? She tugged at her ear lobe, trying to group her thoughts.

His head wobbled in a circular motion as if he couldn't decide whether to shake or nod. "Perhaps I had allowed it to come to that. But I've since realized I was not being fair."

"You realize the majority of the people in France have little say in the government or the military."

"Yes. I do. I have always known that. But after a time, I saw enough hate it was easy to push that belief aside and assume the opposite."

She let out a breath. "I thought it might only be me you did not like. I am relieved to know that is not the case."

He looked away from her, his brow creasing.

Nodding, she pinched her lips shut. She *had* believed correctly, then. It was in part her that he did not like initially. Gabby hated how much it hurt to know that particular fact. "What was it about me you disliked from the very first moment?"

She watched him as he watched the flames. He was quiet for a long time.

Gabby pushed off the couch. "I see. Then I shall bother you no more." She turned, proud she had kept the hurt out of her voice. Clutching her book to her chest, she turned toward the door. When had she opened herself up to be hurt by this man? She closed her eyes, afraid she was too late to close herself off now.

His hand wrapped lightly around her wrist, and she looked down. A tingling sensation danced across her skin and up her arm. It was as she feared. She *was* too late to protect herself.

"Please, wait." His voice was soft, as was his hand still holding onto her arm. "Let me explain."

She allowed him to tug her back to the sofa, dropping down closer to him than she'd been before. She bit her lip, trying not to let his closeness distract her. "What is there to explain?" She reluctantly pulled her arm from his hand, scowling down at the spot his hand had vacated. The skin still tingled, but the warmth was gone. She needed to put a stop to these errant feelings. As she had just discovered, she would only be hurt if she allowed them to continue.

"I'm aware that not all the people in France agreed with the Republic and Napoleon. I know many people, mostly in the countryside, felt removed from what was happening—at least until the armies arrived. Suddenly they were thrust into something they did not want and in some cases did not believe in." His voice remained low.

She nodded. She and her father had been among those people. While her father had not much cared for her mother's family, he had been sickened by their executions. From the time of the revolution onward, he'd been at odds with those governing. Not that he had spoken openly about it. He was smart enough to see that would come to nothing good. But as Gabby grew older, in the quiet of their parlor he would share his concerns—concerns she found she shared.

"I believed one of those people was a woman named Mireille. She came to our camp, cursing Napoleon and all his men. She said when the French soldiers came through ahead of us, they had killed her father because he would not give them his last cow." He took a deep breath, his brow creasing and his head shaking. His eyes stayed focused on the flames licking at the log in the grate. "I should have investigated her more thoroughly, but she seemed so sincere and truthful. And she was a woman. I had not yet learned that should not matter." He shrugged. "She was young, although not so young and unprotected as I originally thought."

A corner of Gabby's mouth lifted. She knew what he was not saying. "You mean she was pretty."

He smirked. "Yes. She was that. But that was not the reason we believed her." His protest was emphatic. Perhaps a little too emphatic. "At least, it was not for me. I truly believed what she told us."

Gabby knew what came next in this story. "But it was all a lie, was it not? A trick to get close to you so she could send information back to the French army." Gabby had heard several tales of a similar nature. It was not uncommon for French generals to seek out pretty, young girls to use as spies.

He nodded. "Her deceit cost many men their lives."

She frowned. "What has this to do with me? I was never a spy."

"No." His voice was hollow. "But you sound like her. When I first heard you, that day at the fair, it brought back memories—memories I never wanted to think on again." His head shook slowly, his thumb rubbing firmly on the back of his other hand.

Gabby watched as it went from red then to white and back to red.

"The inflections and tone of your voice? It's eerily close to Mireille's." He glanced up at her. "I am not the only one who has noticed."

"Mr. Perkins." That was why the man had treated her with such disdain.

"Yes."

She twisted the tip of her little finger. What was she to do? How was she to stay in a country that hated her for nothing she had done or had any control over? It would be easy to dismiss if it was only Aaron and Mr. Perkins whose good opinion she had lost. Unfortunately, it was more common than not. And she could not blame the woman, Mireille, in all the cases of her mistreatment. For many people, it *was* simply that she was French.

Peter had said there may be some who held her nationality against her. But he'd said most would accept her. Gabby had not found many of those people. Besides Peter and Caroline, Lord and Lady Kirtley and their family had been the only people to truly accept her. Could she add Aaron to that list?

She sunk into the pillows behind her. It seemed a lost cause.

"But that was before I knew you." Aaron placed a hand on her arm, his face creased with concern. "Now I see very little of Mireille in you."

Gabby smirked. "But you still see some?" That was not very encouraging.

"Yes. But the similarities are few."

"What are they?" She straightened her back. Perhaps she could change those things that were not desirable to an English gentleman. She would have to if she wished to have a successful Season.

"You are French." He grinned.

"Yes. This is true." Her voice was bland. He was teasing her.

He ticked the similarities off on his fingers. "You are young and beautiful."

She held his gaze. "You think I am beautiful?" She should not have said it out loud, and if she was not so happy about it, she would have chided herself. Her mouth turned up, but she pushed it back down. If she smiled now, he would think all was well. But it wasn't. At least not yet. She wanted to know if there were any other similarities which were less desirable than the ones he had listed. Did he think her deceitful? She did not know if she could stay at Ivydale a moment longer if that was his opinion of her.

"Is there more?"

He shook his head. "No. The similarities end there." His voice was soft and sounded sincere. He gave her arm a gentle squeeze.

Her backbone melted, and her chest tightened.

"I know you are not her, Gabrielle." He picked up the book she'd been reading. "*Les Contemporaines.* Are you enjoying it?"

Gabby blinked a few times, her brain trying to catch up to the quick change of subjects. "Er. Yes. My papa had several volumes, but not this one. It is very good."

He smiled. "I am happy for it. Do you have a favorite story?"

She shook her head. It seemed their previous conversation had come to an end. Gabby was not certain she had received all the answers to her questions. But she believed she could be content for now. "I do not know yet. I will not know until after I have finished and put it down for the day."

He looked at her, his head tilted at an angle, eyes wide with questions. "Why must you wait so long to discover a favorite?"

She lifted a shoulder. "When I finish reading, the story that keeps coming to my mind—the one that I cannot stop thinking about—that is the story that will be my favorite."

His head slowly nodded. "Ah. Yes. That makes perfect sense."

He turned slightly. "Perhaps once you have finished, we can come back to this discussion. I am interested in your thoughts."

"Why?" Why would he care what she thought about a book? Why would he care what she thought about anything?

"Because I think you are an intelligent woman. It has been a long time since I could have a conversation with someone about these books."

A warmth spread through her. That would mean spending more time with him. She knew it was unwise to get excited about the prospect—the weather could change at any time and they would leave for Dovehaven—but she could not help herself.

It had been ages since she had conversed in French about a French book. She glanced up at Aaron. That it would be with him only increased her excitement.

CHAPTER 12

Rebekah had only left her rooms a few times since St. Stephen's Day. And then she'd been subdued, avoiding Aaron's gaze and only speaking when asked a question directly.

Aaron knew it was his doing. The set down he'd given her had not had the desired effect. Or perhaps it had. She was no longer suggesting the notion of marriage. But he regretted that he had made her feel the need to remain secluded. It seemed as if there was no correct solution where Rebekah was concerned.

He frowned into the mirror as Martin brushed at his coat. Perhaps he should speak with her, at least try to eliminate the awkwardness when they were in the same room.

He tugged on the front of his coat, pulling it tightly over his chest. He'd hoped to have some information back from his solicitor before he'd had this conversation—hoped to have some kind of plan to offer to her. But maybe he should not wait for news before speaking with her.

"Thank you, Martin."

"You are welcome, my lord." The valet bowed and moved to clear the room of Aaron's nightclothes.

Aaron walked straight to his study, intent on summoning Rebekah as soon as he thought her awake and fed. He'd barely sat down when a knock sounded, and Collins entered the room. "The messenger you sent to London has returned, my lord." He held out a folded paper. "This is the reply."

Aaron smiled. The timing couldn't be better. That did not happen often. Perhaps it was a sign that he was on the right path—not that he was a superstitious man.

He would hold off meeting with Rebekah until he read what Mr. Blakely had to say.

"Thank you, Collins." He cracked the wax seal and unfolded the letter. Seeing his solicitor's cramped writing brought back the memory of reading the letter telling him of Henry's death. Aaron's heartbeat hammered in his chest. It had been the worst letter he'd ever received—even more so than the news of his father's death.

He paused and controlled his breathing. Hopefully, this would have better news.

My Lord,

I found your letter of December twenty-third interesting, indeed. As your brother's widow, Lady Brinton's jointure is small (a mere three hundred and thirty pounds). Of this she is aware. Do not let her lead you to believe otherwise.

Aaron paused. Had he given his solicitor the wrong idea about Rebekah? She'd not been acting as Henry described her, but Aaron did not believe her deceitful. He rather hoped, once he had answers to give her, that she would become the woman Henry had described in his letters once again. Aaron returned his attention to Mr. Blakely's words.

As to your other question—there are three other Brinton properties, besides Ivydale. None may be sold or given away outright, however their use is left to your discretion. I have enclosed a list of the properties along with their location, advantages and disadvantages as I see them.

I am at your service however you wish to proceed.

Yours,

Robert Blakely

Aaron leaned back in his chair. Rebekah's jointure was even more dismal than he'd thought. It was no wonder she was anxious about her future. He shifted his chair to the side, leaning heavily on the arm, and stared out the window. It also explained why she might think marrying Aaron was her only option. How had Henry been so careless as to leave Rebekah with so little?

He lifted the second paper from the letter and looked down the list. Heatherbrook in Shropshire, Payne Manor in Essex, and Peterfeld cottage in Somerset. Hmm. He rubbed at his chin.

He'd forgotten about Peterfeld. It had been decades since he'd last been there. The cottage was markedly smaller than the dower house here on Ivydale, but not so small as to be looked down upon. And it was within easy distance of Bath.

Did a single woman need much more than a small cottage with a handful of servants? Especially one who'd come from such humble beginnings. But if he was to offer Peterfeld to Rebekah, he needed to speak to his mother about it first.

From his remembrance, they'd only been to Peterfeld once because his mother had found it lacking—in every respect. Every time they'd been to Bath, they had let a townhouse on the Royal Crescent rather than stay at the family's cottage. "It is not big enough for one of us, much less the family." He could hear her voice as if it were yesterday. But his mother had always had rather lofty expectations. Aaron did not suspect Rebekah would be so dismissive of the place. It was—or had been—well cared for and was quite grand for its size.

Regardless of his mother's stated feelings for the cottage, if Aaron offered it to Rebekah without speaking to his mother first, she would undoubtedly discover fond memories of the place, such that she could not let it go.

He stood and walked over to the bell pull. There was also the option of just increasing Rebekah's jointure—giving her a certain amount per annum until she remarried. Aaron was confident Rebekah would remarry—someone other than himself—before too long.

A maid knocked on the partially opened door. She curtsied. "You rang, m'lord?"

"Yes, would you please send someone to the dower house for my mother? I need to speak with her immediately."

The girl dipped her head. "Right away, m'lord."

Aaron ran a hand through his hair. Now if his mother would just get here, he could get this whole situation with Rebekah finished.

Aaron sat behind his desk as he waited for Rebekah. He would be more comfortable in a chair by the fire, but he felt the need for a buffer, just in case flirty Rebekah came to the meeting. It also hid his bouncing knee.

He was not nervous about the meeting as much as he was uncertain of how Rebekah would react to his offers. He feared there would be tears at some point, and he didn't handle watering pots well.

A knock sounded on the door and he jumped, his bouncing knee knocking against the bottom of his desk's center drawer. "Come."

Rebekah's face peered into the room. "You asked to see me, my lord?"

He should smile, set her at ease, but he did not want to give her false hope. What if she would only be happy with marriage? The notion felt arrogant, but a small part of him worried that Rebekah just did not wish to ever give up the title of Lady Brinton. Regardless, marriage was not something he was willing to entertain.

Based on Rebekah's creased brow, he must have given her more of a grimace than something that provided any sense of reassurance. "Yes, Lady Brinton. Please, do come in."

Her steps were tentative, her gaze glancing around the room as if checking for people lurking in the corners and dark spaces.

He motioned to the chair across from him, the chair his mother had vacated not more than an hour earlier. Thankfully, she had not claimed a preference for Peterfeld, giving Aaron leave to offer it as a solution to Rebekah's problem.

He took a deep breath and leaned forward, placing his forearms on the desk and intertwining his fingers. "Lady Brinton, I understand your anxiety, of late, regarding your future." He raised a brow. "I believe we discussed your idea, but as I pointed out, it is fraught with problems."

Her face pinked, and she dropped her gaze to her lap. Aaron hoped this meant she had finally seen the error in her thinking.

"We need not discuss that point again. As I promised, I have come up with several options for you to choose from."

She lifted her gaze. Equal parts hope and fear filled her eyes.

"Under normal circumstances, the dower house would be yours to use. However, since my mother still lives, that option is not available." He glanced down at the missive from Mr. Blakely. "I have received a letter from my solicitor and from his information I can offer you the following options." He captured her gaze in his. "You have time to consider these options. I will return to London for the Season after Twelfth Night and shall be at Larkspur House until Parliament adjourns. You have until then to see to your new arrangements."

She nodded, even as her lip trembled. It still surprised him this woman before him was the same shameless flirt he had been dealing with for more than a week.

He reached for a paper on his desk. "I can offer you five thousand pounds above your current jointure. You would receive it as a onetime payment and could do with it what you wish. But it would require you to seek a different residence."

Her eyes widened, but he did not know if it was for good or bad. Was she happy with the first option?

"The second would give you an additional five hundred pounds per annum—as long as you are unmarried. This option would also require you to seek another residence."

Her lips parted. Drat, the woman's emotions were hard to understand.

"The last option would not add to your jointure, however, it would provide you with a residence, and staff, until you remarry."

Her lower jaw now nearly rested on her chest. "Where is the house?"

"In Somerset. Charlcombe to be precise."

"That is near Bath, is it not?" Rebekah twisted her hands in her lap. She looked back up at Aaron. "Why are you sending me so far away? Why can I not stay here?"

Aaron sighed. "You know why, Lady Brinton." He rotated his head right and left. Why was she making this so difficult? He was doing his best to provide for her. He owed Henry that much.

"I would be living there alone?" She licked her lips.

Aaron nodded. "You would have several staff and your maid with you. If you wished, I am certain we could arrange for a companion also." Would those provisions make her happy?

Rebekah ran her hands down the front of her skirt. "You said I can think on it?"

He nodded. "Indeed. This is not a decision to be made hastily. I hope you will think about it in depth. If you wish, write your father and ask his opinion."

She stood up and moved behind the chair, placing her hands on the back. "I do appreciate all you have done." Her voice hitched. "I shall do as you advise and write to my father to ask for his guidance." She pointed to the papers on his desk. "May I have a copy of my options? I should like to give my father accurate sums."

Aaron picked up the paper and handed it to her. "If you have questions, please ask. I am at your service."

She managed a shaky smile.

Aaron forced himself not to frown. Why was she still so

emotional? Had he not given her three very generous offers—offers far beyond what was required for his brother's widow?

"Thank you, my lord." She bowed and turned toward the door.

Once it was closed firmly behind her, Aaron let out a sigh. It seemed anything less than marriage would not be acceptable in her eyes. The woman was destined to be disappointed.

He pushed out of his chair and walked to the floor-to-ceiling windows at the far side of the room. An icy breeze blew between the sash and the frame, the panes frosted around the edges.

He hated this harsh weather. Normally, even at this time of year, he'd be able to go for a ride and clear his head. But now, the air was so frigid he feared what it would do to Bruce's lungs.

He clasped his hands behind his back. What was he to do instead? He grinned. Perhaps he should peruse the library.

CHAPTER 13

Gabby entered the sitting room, intent on finishing the blanket she was stitching for Peter and Caroline's baby. If they ever were to have one. She knew no one else to give it to. Not so urgent a task without an actual babe on the way, but the snow left little else to do today.

Lady Brinton already occupied the settee closest to the fire, her head bowed low as she focused on her own sampler.

Gabby quietly made her way to the couch opposite.

Lady Brinton had not come down to dinner the previous evening, crying off because of a headache. Seeing her here this morning surely meant she was feeling better.

Gabby sat down and removed the blanket from her sewing basket.

Lady Brinton sighed and bent her head lower, muttering as she picked out several stitches.

Gabby placed several stitches in the blanket on her lap, stopping frequently to glance at the lady from under her lashes. This woman was a mystery. One day she was openly pursuing a match with Aaron and the next she was as quiet as a church mouse.

Lady Brinton scowled down at the fabric, yanking at the thread.

"Pardon me. Are you well, Lady Brinton?"

She looked up, her scowl staying firmly in place. "I am perfectly well. Do not concern yourself on my account."

Gabby studied the lady, recognizing the look of fear and desperation in Lady Brinton's eyes.

Gabby had seen that same look many times reflected from the mirror after her father's death. It had come from the knowledge that she didn't know what her future held, what was to become of her. She could guess the lady had similar concerns. A widow, especially one who had not produced an heir, was generally in a precarious situation unless her husband had provided for her.

Gabby pinched her lips together. Certainly, Lady Brinton's husband had done so. Gabby looked around the finely decorated room. Money was not lacking at Ivydale.

She half-turned her attention back to the blanket. Was there anything she could say that would help the lady? Would Lady Brinton allow Gabby to be her friend?

"I realize I am speaking out of turn, but I understand how you are feeling. If you wish to talk to someone, I am a good listener." Gabby pretended to look at her needlework, wanting the comment to feel casual and carefree.

A mirthless laugh escaped Lady Brinton's lips. "You know nothing of how I feel. You've come here, all too eager to take one of the few eligible men from the deserving ladies of English descent." She sneered. "Do not pretend to know my feelings."

Gabby swallowed. Perhaps it would be better to leave this be, to let the lady suffer on her own. She had just made it obvious that she did not want Gabby's friendship.

Staring at the deep green thread, Gabby formed the leaf of the flower she stitched. What she wouldn't have given to have someone to confide in while she was struggling. Even with her new friendship with Eleanor, Gabby still did not feel comfortable in confiding everything to her, at least not yet.

"I know what it is to lie in bed at night, unable to sleep for fear of what will happen when I awake the next day." She sighed. "I know what it is to have no notion if I shall have money enough to provide for my needs or if a workhouse is the only option. I know uncertainty."

"How could you know such things?" She raked her eyes over Gabby. "You do not look as if you've suffered a day in your life."

"I could say the same for you, my lady. But you do not know my story, just as I do not fully know yours. But that does not mean we do not share some similarities."

Lady Brinton set her sampler in her lap. "Oh, pray tell. What similarities could we possibly have? Have you lost your husband, the only man you have ever loved?"

Gabby shook her head. "No, but I lost my father—the only family I had left and the only person ever to love me."

Lady Brinton snapped her mouth shut. "How did you come to live with Lord and Lady Kirtley?"

"Lord Rockwell—he is Lady Kirtley's brother— lived with my father and me for several years when I was a girl. He promised my father that should anything happen, he would become my guardian until I wed." Gabby took a deep breath, dropping her stitchery into her lap. "I left my country for one I'd never seen—one that is at war with my homeland. I had not seen Peter in half a decade, and I had no notion if he would accept me or even remember his promise. For all I knew, his circumstances had changed, and he was no longer in a position to be my guardian." She remembered those feelings of uncertainty as if they were yesterday—perhaps because she still had moments of unease.

Gabby picked up the blanket. "I very much would have liked to have a friend during those times. I had thought perhaps you may, as well. But I can see I was wrong. I apologize for bothering you."

Lady Brinton was silent, but she did not resume her sewing. "You are not wrong." Her voice was quiet and strained. "I am the one who should apologize. I was terribly rude."

"Perhaps we could start again?" Gabby raised smiling eyes to her.

Lady Brinton nodded. "I don't deserve your friendship, but I should like it, nonetheless."

Gabby set her blanket to the side and stood up, walking around the low table between the two couches. "Lady Brinton, it is a pleasure to meet you. My name is Gabrielle Babineaux but as I can see we are to become dearest friends, you may call me Gabby."

Lady Brinton stood and dipped her head. "The pleasure is all mine, Gabby. I would very much like it if you called me Rebekah."

Gabby returned to her seat and picked up her blanket. "That is a lovely name. Is it from the bible?"

Rebekah nodded. "My father is a vicar. All of his children have biblical names."

Gabby grinned. She rather liked that idea. Perhaps when she had children, she would do the same.

"Gabby, how did you do it? At times I feel as if the uncertainty will swallow me up and I shall never climb back out." Her voice hitched.

"It was difficult, but what choice did I have? If I only worried about what would happen to me that day, it was easier to manage. And I did what I could to make a future for myself. I set out for England knowing little of how I would be received. I am fortunate things turned out like they did."

Rebekah pulled a folded paper from her pocket. "When I married Henry, I could not have been happier. We were very fond of each other and lived happily. I never imagined he would die so young. As the daughter of a vicar, you can imagine my dowry was small. My father negotiated with Henry's solicitor for my jointure. Henry was in good health; no one imagined I should need a jointure for some time." She looked down at the paper. "I realize it was Mr. Blakely's duty to make the best arrangements on Henry's behalf, but was he not to be my solicitor also? Should he not have looked out for my interests as well?" She sighed and her face pinked. "I will not be living in poverty with what was allocated, but nearly." She grimaced and looked down at the paper again. "I felt desperate which led me to behave in ways that are not my nature, hoping to secure my future any way I could. I am rather ashamed of myself now."

A burning sensation flared up in Gabby's stomach as she remembered the flirtatious woman she'd seen when she first arrived at Ivydale. This woman did not resemble that one in the least but still, her stomach churned.

"Aaron will not consider my plans for the future, but he has given me other options."

Gabby's body sagged back against the sofa. Was she saying Aaron had refused her advances? She had not thought him interested in Rebekah, but the relief surging through her now made her realized there was a small part of her which thought she may be wrong.

Rebekah handed the paper across the table. "I have written to my father to ask for his advice, but I truly do not know what is best and I do not know if I can wait for his answer."

Gabby tied off the last stitch and reached for the paper, looking it over. The sums listed looked generous, but she was not very knowledgeable about what it cost to run a household. "I wish I could offer my advice, but I have little to give on this matter." She handed the paper back. "Perhaps you could consult Lady Kirtley?"

Rebekah shook her head. "It is no longer the sums that concern me, either of these will allow me a comfortable life. It is finding my place wherever I go. Do I return to Bedfordshire and find a home near my parents or accept the cottage near Bath?" She folded the paper and slipped it in the cuff of her sleeve. "I believe Lord Brinton thinks me to remarry quickly. But I have already found a love match once. Can one hope to find that twice in a lifetime? Or am I resigned to marry for convenience?"

Gabby frowned. "Must you remarry at all?"

Rebekah shrugged. "What am I if not someone's wife?"

While Gabby did not like the notion, she did not have an answer for it. "I'm sorry, but I do not know."

"Nor do I, which is why I am uncertain which option is best."

Rebekah laid aside her sampler and straightened her back. "Until Aaron returns from London once Parliament adjourns, I am still mistress of this house and I intend to do my duty. I have heard Mrs. Perkins is soon to have her baby. I was to visit her today. Would you care to join me?"

Mrs. Perkins? While she had seemed nice enough to Gabby, her husband had not. Knowing what Rebekah did not, Gabby did not feel comfortable visiting the cottages, especially without Aaron.

Still, it thrilled Gabby that Rebekah was asking her to visit a tenant. Was that not a genuine gesture of friendship?

"I should love to, but I believe Mr. Perkins will not welcome me." She glanced down at the blanket. "But I have only just finished this blanket. Perhaps you could give it to her?"

"Mr. Perkins is a gruff man, but he has never been unkind to me."

"Yes, but you do not have a French accent."

Rebekah nodded in understanding. "Ah. Perhaps it *would* be best if you did not go." Rebekah's eyes lit, and she clapped her hands together. "I nearly forgot. He will be helping in the stables today. It is a chore he does to earn his rent during the winter months. He will not be at home, which means you can come. Mrs. Perkins will love the blanket, I'm sure of it."

Gabby bit the inside of her cheek. She still was not at ease with the notion, but Rebekah seemed confident he would not be home. Perhaps it would not be a problem if she went.

"Very well; if he will not be home, I should love to visit Mrs. Perkins."

Rebekah brightened and Gabby finally saw the woman that had piqued Aaron's brother's interest. "Come, we will need to change into warmer clothes if we are to walk in this weather."

They walked as far as the landing before separating to go to their own rooms.

Gabby dressed quickly, feeling lighter than she had in weeks. Rebekah was her first genuine friend, except for maybe Caroline and now Eleanor—but they felt more like older sisters than friends.

Even while Gabby had been in London with the Kirtleys, no other young ladies had taken the time to become friends with her. She suspected Rebekah was not the only one who'd felt Gabby was trying to take something—or someone—she had no right to. She suspected it was the reason she and Miss Carter were at constant odds with each other.

Lady Brinton was not the only person here who needed a friend.

Gabby hurried back to the sitting room to retrieve the baby blanket she had finished embroidering. She wrapped the blanket in some tissue she'd found in her trunk.

When she got to the entryway, Rebekah was already waiting for her. "Are you ready?"

Gabby slipped on her pelisse and quickly tied her bonnet. "Yes. I'm sorry to have kept you waiting."

Rebekah waved her comment aside. "I have only been here a moment." She turned toward the doors. "The snow has let up. Let's go before it starts again."

They followed the path toward the cottages. Thankfully others had already made the journey back and forth so the snow was fairly packed, keeping it from coming over the tops of Gabby's half-boots. The trees and hedges sparkled, as the sun peeked through a small break in the clouds. Gabby held her hand up to her eyes. "It is so bright. I had nearly forgotten what it was like to be out of doors."

Rebekah sucked in a deep breath. "Yes. It is nice, isn't it?"

They arrived at the Perkins' cottage and Rebekah knocked on the door. Mrs. Perkins answered. She smiled at the two ladies as she curtsied slightly. "Good day, Lady Brinton." She nodded to Gabby but did not greet her.

"And good day to you." Rebekah motioned to Gabby. "I do not believe you have met my dear friend, Miss Babineaux."

Mrs. Perkins shook her head. "She came with Lord Brinton to deliver the St. Stephen's Day gift—very generous it was—but he did not make introductions." Mrs. Perkins nodded again. "Miss Babineaux."

"We came to inquire after you. That babe is to arrive soon, is it not?" Lady Brinton dropped her eyes to the woman's abdomen.

Mrs. Perkins rubbed a hand over her belly. "Yes. It should be any day now."

Rebekah thrust a package into the woman's hands and Gabby followed suit.

"We wanted you to have these before the babe came."

Gabby wiggled her toes in her boots, trying to relieve the prickling of cold in the soles of her feet.

"Thank ye, my lady. It is very kind of ye to think of us."

Rebekah nodded. "Miss Babineaux stitched the blanket."

Mrs. Perkins looked slightly uncomfortable at the gift from a near stranger. "Thank you, Miss Babineaux."

"You are most welcome." Gabby rubbed her hands up and down her arms slowly. "I hope it keeps the baby warm." She paused. Dare she mention the herbs? "When the time comes, I know of some herbs that may help you deliver more comfortably."

The woman looked at her like she didn't believe Gabby could know anything of the sort.

"I discovered them when my father was ill. They seemed to help." Why was she still prattling on? The woman obviously did not desire Gabby's help.

A thumping sounded, and the door flew open. Mr. Perkins's face appeared at the door. He smiled when he looked at Lady Brinton, but the smile quickly faded when he spied Gabby. "What is *she* doing here, Patience?"

Gabby took two steps back.

"Which one is from her?" He motioned to the parcels in his wife's hands.

She lifted the tissue-wrapped gift from Gabby and he yanked it from her. "We don't want your gifts." He threw the blanket on the snowy ground at Gabby's feet. "Meaning no disrespect to you, my lady," he said to Rebekah, "but the Frog is not welcome." He turned and moved back into the house. "What's the major thinking, allowing a spy to stay in his 'ouse?" he muttered.

Rebekah let out a gasp. "Mr. Perkins!"

Gabby bit the side of her cheek to stop herself from crying. Slowly, she stooped and gathered up the package, the tissue paper dripping in her hands. Was this only because of that Mireille woman Aaron had told her about?

Her hands shook. This had been a mistake. She should never have made this trip with Rebekah.

Mrs. Perkins held up a hand. "Please, my lady. Just go. It will only make things worse," she whispered; she closed the door without uttering a proper goodbye.

"I have never—" Rebekah sputtered. "Even when I was only a vicar's daughter I have never been treated so abominably. I have a mind to speak with Aaron and demand he remove that man from the property." Rebekah looped her arm through Gabby's, pulling her close.

"Please Rebekah, do not mention this to Lord Brinton." This was her fault, not Mr. Perkins. Gabby knew his opinion of her and still she had come.

"And why should I not?" Rebekah looked wide-eyed at Gabby. "That man was dreadful."

She sighed. "Mr. Perkins was one of Lord Brinton's men. I am sure he saw many terrible things in the war and is only reacting out of fear. I will only be here a short time. There is no reason to make that man and his family leave. Especially not in this weather and with a babe on the way." Gabby paused. "Is he dangerous do you think?"

"He blusters a bit, but I do not believe he would harm anyone. Besides, Aaron told Henry to collect both his and Mr. Millard's weapon's as a condition of their lease. Our gamekeeper provides them with meat." She glanced back at the cottages and raised a brow. "But you may be right. Now is not the time to force them off the land. But Aaron should know how Mr. Perkins treated us."

Gabby squeezed Rebekah's arm against her body. If there was no danger, why must Aaron be made aware? "Please. Summer will come and we will both be gone. I will simply stay away from the tenant cottages until I leave."

Rebekah narrowed her eyes. "I do not agree with your silence. But I will not tell Aaron of this incident if you oppose it." She sighed. "And thank you for reminding me of my impending departure."

Gabby exhaled. "It is a reality for us both. Should we not embrace it?"

"I should have preferred a few days more of peace before I had to think on it, but I suppose you are correct. I should accept the notion of leaving."

Gabby knew exactly how Rebekah felt. The thoughts of leaving Ivydale held less appeal with each passing day.

CHAPTER 14

Aaron leaned back against the settee, his book in his lap. A noise sounded in the corridor and he looked up at the door. Was she coming? He stared for several moments before he accepted that no one was coming.

He huffed out a breath. He had been sitting in the library pretending to read for more than an hour waiting for Gabrielle.

She seemed to spend as much time as she could in this room, except for today, when he was hoping to find her here.

He looked at the book in his lap but saw none of the words on the page. The door opened and Aaron shot to his feet, smiling widely. The maid who entered took a step back when she saw him.

His body slumped. Where the devil was she? He should just go in search of her. But what would he tell her when he discovered her? That was why he'd come to the library. He did not need an excuse to be in the library, but if he sought her out, what would he say was his reason?

The maid curtsied. "Begging your pardon, my lord. I can come back later."

Aaron raised a hand. "No. I will leave. I am finished in here anyhow." He tossed the book on the side table. Maybe he should just retire to his study. The staff would not be doing the end-of-year cleaning in that room. Perhaps then he could think of a reason to seek out Gabrielle.

He strode down the corridor and into his study, stopping midstride on his way to his desk. Rebekah sat on the sofa next to the fire. How long had she been in here? Could it be she was doing the same thing he had been doing only a moment ago? Waiting for a specific person to arrive in the room?

He cleared his throat. "Rebekah. I was not expecting you. I'm sorry if I have kept you waiting."

She shook her head. "I was just thinking and waiting. I hope you are not angry with me for invading your study, but it seems to be the only room not subject to a flurry of cleaning."

Aaron chuckled. "Yes, I noticed that as well." He motioned to the couch. "Please, stay."

Rebekah stood up, the hand at her side rubbing back and forth at a fold in her gown. "I wished to speak to you if you have a moment."

Aaron stifled a sigh. He wanted to tell her he did not have the time, but that would have been a lie. It would also mean he had to make himself look busy. And he really had no notion of what he would do. He had finished going through all the ledgers and his meeting with Mr. Babcock, his bailiff, was days off.

Besides, ledgers and matters of the estate were not what had been occupying his mind. He motioned to the chair in front of his desk.

"Would you mind terribly if we sat by the fire? I cannot seem to get warm today." Rebekah had not moved even a step away from her seat. She sat down on the settee.

Aaron eyed the safety of his desk but nodded as he turned back toward the fireplace. "Certainly. Your comfort is of the utmost importance." He grimaced at the slight tone of sarcasm in his voice. He glanced at Rebekah, but she did not seem to have noticed.

He lowered himself into the winged back chair opposite

Rebekah. He was less leery of her now that she acted with some decorum. "What did you wish to talk to me about?"

She swallowed. "I have made my decision regarding which option I should prefer." She rubbed her hands together in her lap.

"It has only been a few days. You need not decide yet. I thought I had made myself clear on that."

She nodded. "Yes, you did. It is not for you that I have decided quickly, but for me." She studied her thumbnail. "Until I make my choice, I believe I will feel unsettled. I realize I must move on with my life. I know you gave me until summer, but I believe I will leave as soon as the weather warms enough for me to travel safely."

Aaron glanced out the window. "It could be June before that happens."

Rebekah grinned. "Yes, I know."

"What have you decided then?" He leaned forward, placing his elbows on his knees. He truly did not care which option she picked, but he believed the house near Bath would be best for her. It would put her in proximity to society, even if it was smaller than that in London. And it would also allow her to use her small jointure for personal things, rather than to let a house and pay the wages of the servants.

Her face brightened. "I have wish to take the cottage in Charlcombe." Her frame relaxed as if just saying the words had eased all her anxiety.

Aaron smiled and steepled his fingers in front of his chin. "I think it a good decision. Did your father agree?"

She shook her head. "I have not yet heard from him, but I am confident in my choice." A heavy breath pushed from her lips.

"If you change your mind, you need only come talk to me. Once the snow shows signs of letting up for good, I will send a note to the caretaker of Peterfeld and inform him of your plans. He should have the place ready and staffed by the time you arrive in the spring."

She took a deep cleansing breath. "That would be lovely. Thank you, Aaron."

He dipped his head. This was the woman he had pictured after reading Henry's letters. He was glad she had returned.

"And Aaron?"

He raised a brow in question.

"You asserted, once, that it was only Henry who had made a love match. That is not true. I loved him very much and you will never know how much it pained me to pretend otherwise. But I could see no other option." Her lips quivered slightly. "Thank you for providing one." She pushed herself up and hurried from the room.

Aaron winced. In thinking back on the exchange, he had not been kind in his words. He could excuse his behavior with hers, but in truth, he should have realized she was acting out of desperation.

And now she had fled before he'd even been able to stand, let alone offer a proper apology.

He glanced at the open door. Perhaps he would give her some time before he invaded her privacy to do so. He could find her this evening or in the morning.

He sat back and dropped his hands into his lap. He was back to the problem of having nothing to do. He rubbed a hand over the old wound in his shoulder, exhaustion seeping into his bones. Perhaps he should lie down and rest.

He moved to the couch and kicked off his Wellingtons before unbuttoning his tailcoat and tossing it onto the chair. Grabbing a cushion, he tucked it under his head and relaxed. His eyes drifted closed just as a flurry of voices carried down the corridor.

What the devil was going on? It must be the Kirtley children, though where they were going, he could not guess. The roads were still quite impassible.

Several laughs carried over the top of the voices.

Aaron grunted and slung his arm over his eyes. Surely the noise would die down if he gave it a moment.

Sure enough, the voices receded and quiet again filled the house. He sighed and snuggled a little deeper into the cushions. The fire crackled, and he rotated his neck several times, allowing his eyes to drift shut.

Something smashed into the window, and Aaron jumped to his feet, sleep pushed from his mind. Voices and laughter sounded just outside. He looked over to the window, ensuring the glass had not broken. Slush and bits of snow formed a watery path down the pane until it stopped at the grille.

Aaron grumbled as he walked to the window and peered out. He longed for the deep slumber he'd enjoyed before going off to the continent to fight. It was the Kirtley children...and Gabrielle. So the nursery was where she'd been hiding. He should have realized that sooner.

He grinned, his earlier fatigue and irritation gone, and the sudden urge for snow games gripped him. He padded across the room and yanked on his boots. Perhaps this snow was good for something after all.

Aaron stopped at the corner of the house, peering around as he fastened the last button on his greatcoat. The children, even the little one, ran about the grounds, scooping up snow and tossing it at each other. Aaron raised a brow. Was the governess even taking part?

He had seen little of her since their arrival, but from his brief observations, she had appeared rather stiff. He would never have expected her to participate in such activities.

Gabrielle stayed with the littlest child, blocking any snow thrown in her direction. The girl laughed, picking up snow in her small hands and throwing it over Gabrielle's shoulder. Or rather, she *tried* to throw it over Gabrielle's shoulder, but the little girl was not quite tall enough—even in Gabrielle's seated position—and the snow splattered against Gabrielle's pelisse.

"Babby, Babby." The little girl clapped and yelled as Gabrielle packed the snow tight in her hand and handed it off to the tot.

Gabrielle then formed her own snowball. She threw it and thumped the Kirtley boy between the shoulders.

He turned, eyes wide, and scooped up snow in his hand as he changed course and headed for Gabrielle. She gathered the little one up in her arms, shrieking with laughter as she took off at a run.

"You cannot escape me, Gabby," he hollered as he released the snowball and sent it flying toward her.

Gabby? Was that what the boy had called her?

Hmm. He studied her while his presence was still unknown. Gabby. The name was short and concise. It fit her somehow.

Aaron kneeled and filled both hands with snow. Pressing them together, he formed a tight ball. He saw Gabby duck behind a large bush, the little girl huddled behind her. Little giggles sounded and Gabby placed her finger to her lips. "Shh, Sophie. We don't want them to hear us."

If he snuck through the herb garden, he could come at the bush from behind. She would never see him coming. He grinned.

Sophia's little gloved hands covered her own mouth. "Shhh," she repeated.

Aaron moved wide, using a row of hedges for cover until he slipped into the garden. With all of the herbs now covered in snow, there was little to hide behind, but the children were yelling and shrieking enough to mask his steps. Crouching low, he came in behind the bush Gabby huddled behind. "Gabby, you are missing out on the fun, hiding behind this bush."

Her head whipped around, her eyes wide until she spied the smile on his face. "What are you doing out here?"

"I could not sleep through all the ruckus you were making, so I thought to join you instead." He frowned. "Or is this for family only?"

She placed a hand on his arm, and his body warmed. "I'm sorry we woke you." Her brow creased in concern.

He put his hand on top of hers, hoping to delay its removal and shook his head. "I would take a good snowball fight over sleep any time." He winked and held up his ball. "Now, who shall we target first?"

Gabby tucked her mouth into her muffler, but her eyes twinkled with mischief. She peered around the bush. "Winston is about to throw one at Miss Carter. Hurry; hit him before he can strike."

Aaron stood up and threw his snowball. It caught Winston in the upper shoulder.

Winston let out a yelp and pivoted to find where the snowball had come from, but Aaron dropped to his knees quickly.

Gabby giggled. "Did he see you?"

Excitement bubbled up in Aaron's chest and he nearly giggled too. He shook his head. "I do not believe so. But perhaps we should move to a different hideout." He reached out and lifted Sophia onto his back.

She let out a squeal.

Gabby placed her finger to her lips. "Remember to be quiet, kitten."

She turned back to move out from behind the bush when a half a dozen snowballs came hurling toward them.

Sophia slid from his back and scampered to the other side of the bush, as Aaron bent, packing and throwing snowballs as quickly as he could. Their attackers fled before him, but not before they each threw another ball behind the bush.

Gabby lifted her hands in front of her face to block the blows. She shifted her body sideways, but her foot caught on a low laying branch and she lurched forward.

Aaron dropped the snow from his hands and reached for her before she hit the ground.

She grabbed hold of him, her arms wrapping around his abdomen, her feet slipping on the icy layer beneath the new snow.

Aaron tightened his hold on her, enjoying the feel of her in his arms.

Sophia came back from behind the bush, wrapping her arms around Gabby's legs. "Babby."

"Soph—" Gabby called as her legs kicked out behind her and she pushed further into Aaron.

The change in his balance combined with the icy ground sent Aaron's feet askew; though he struggled to stay upright, he eventually slipped, pulling Gabby and Sophia both down with him. They landed in a heap in the snow.

"Ooomph." Aaron landed hard on his back. He opened his eyes and saw Gabby's face a breath away from his.

Her lips parted and Aaron could not help the parting of his own, nor the sigh that escaped them.

A sore backside seemed a small price to pay if this was the result of such a fall. Perhaps he had been amiss in avoiding the snow thus far. The side of his mouth quirked up.

"Oh, I am sorry, my lord." Gabby scrambled to get up, but her legs tangled with the little girl laying in the folds of her skirts.

Sophia giggled and rolled about but moving off did not appear to be in her plans.

"Sophia, kitten, please move off my skirts. I cannot stand until you do." She turned embarrassed eyes on Aaron. "Are you hurt? I should have asked after you earlier."

Aaron nodded, only just restraining himself from reaching up and touching her face. "I have never been better in my life."

Her cheeks looked pinker than they had only moments before. "Soph, please. You must stand up."

Aaron tightened his arms around her, and he felt her breath hitch. She looked back to him.

"Perhaps if we roll over, it will deposit her on the ground next to us." It was the last thing he wanted to do, but he could feel the anxiety building inside her. It was this anxiety that kept him from lifting his head and placing a kiss on her berry-red lips.

"That may be the only way to get her off," Gabby whispered.

Aaron shifted, rolling them both to the side. He heard a soft thud as Sophia landed on the snow. But he did not release Gabby immediately.

She held his gaze as steadily as he held hers. Was she feeling the same draw that he was?

Aaron leaned forward. Had he not given her enough time to disentangle herself from him if she desired it? Did this mean she wanted him to kiss her? He was a gentleman, and a gentleman always obliged a lady her wishes, did he not?

He moved in slowly until he could feel the heat radiating off her cheeks.

"Gabby, are you well? Did we hurt you when we ambushed you just now?"

Gabby jumped to her feet at the sound of Winston's voice. "No. I fell to the ground and Sophia got tangled in my skirts. I am well, as you can see." She snatched Sophia up into her arms and nearly ran from behind the bush.

Aaron rolled to his back, staring up at the gray sky, the sun nowhere in sight. He put his arm over his eyes, allowing the memory of her smell and warm body on his to ward off the cold. But it only lasted a moment. The wet made its way through his coats, down to his skin, gooseflesh raising the hairs on his arms and legs.

He grunted. Now how was he to rid his mind of her? Even as he thought it, he knew he didn't want to be rid of her. The only place he wanted her, besides his mind, was in his arms.

Aaron thought on the way she'd scrambled up and away from him. He sighed. It was highly unlikely he'd ever be that close to her again.

CHAPTER 15

Gabby hurried away from the bush, only allowing Sophia to squirm out of her arms once she had put distance between herself and Aaron. She darted a quick glance over her shoulder. Aaron had not yet emerged from behind the bush.

She bit her bottom lip. Had she hurt him when she'd fallen on top of him? Her cheeks warmed. His smile had seemed to indicate he had not felt any pain.

Had he felt her heart hammering inside her chest? It seemed doubtful he could have missed it. It had thumped as though a drummer boy was pounding out the beat before charging into battle. Although, Gabby suspected hers had a faster cadence than even an experienced drummer could muster.

She turned partially around, debating whether or not she should check on him. She wanted to—almost needed to—until she caught the gaze of Miss Carter.

The lady raised a brow and...smirked? What had she to smirk at Gabby for?

The earlier amusement of the snowball fight faded, and Gabby felt cold. "Come, Soph. It is time for you to rest. I promised Nurse

Jones I would not keep you out of doors for too long." Perhaps she could pass by the bush and check on Aaron on her way back to the house.

She took the little girl's hand and walked toward the side of the house, her gaze flicking frequently to the hideout she had shared with Aaron. Tilting her head, she tried to peer around the tree's snow-covered branches.

A snicker sounded behind her, and Gabby turned to see Miss Carter watching her.

Gabby straightened up and forced herself to look straight ahead. It seemed the lady was intent on embarrassing Gabby. But only Gabby could allow Miss Carter to be successful in her quest. But how did one avoid showing embarrassment?

Gabby swallowed. Perhaps it was merely a matter of perception. Perhaps Miss Carter meant nothing by her smile. Although, that did not ring true considering their history.

Still, Gabby knew what had nearly happened behind that bush, and that caused her discomfiture. She slowed her steps. It seemed more likely the embarrassment was due to how much Gabby wished it had happened, more than anything else.

"Had enough fun, have you?" The warm, gravelly tones washed over her, taking the chill from her body.

Gabby smiled. When had she come to love the sound of his voice? At one time, the sound of his voice had set her hair on end. She dropped Sophia's hand and ran her gloved hand up and down her arm. It appeared her hair still stood on end, though for a completely different reason, now.

"It is time for Sophia to nap."

Gabby could feel Miss Carter's gaze—likely a glare if Gabby had to guess—followed them. She knew why the governess disliked her. Indeed, Miss Carter's displeasure had only seemed to increase since their discussion the other day.

Gabby supposed she should try speaking to Miss Carter again. Surely there was a way for them to be friends. She shook her head.

Why must every association take so much work? And why must Gabby be the one to make all the effort? It was exhausting.

She glanced at the gentleman next to her. If she had learned anything since leaving London, it was that some people's friendship was worth the extra effort.

Sophia pulled Gabby to a stop. "No nap."

Gabby leaned forward and looked Sophia in the eyes. "Did I say nap?" She swatted the words away with her hand. "I must have misspoken. I meant a rest, kitten. I know you do not like naps." She looked up at Aaron and winked.

What? Why had she winked? What kind of lady did such a thing? And to a gentleman, no less?

She dropped her gaze back to Sophia and kept it there as she straightened. They moved toward the house once again and Gabby looked forward, even as her eyes itched to glance over at Aaron.

She tugged on Sophia's hand. "I do not wish for you to catch a cold." Gabby finally allowed herself a quick glance at Aaron from the corner of her eye. Was he mortified at her behavior?

He looked straight ahead, his hands clasped behind his back, but she thought she detected a slight twitch at the corner of his mouth. He did not find her mortifying then, just ridiculous. *Zut.*

Gabby's gaze flicked back to him over and over, taking in a different feature each time. His perfectly angular jaw, his ears, which seemed perfectly proportioned for his head, the way his hair curled over his forehead. It was rare for her to have this much time to watch him without being caught.

She had always thought he was handsome, albeit somewhat grudgingly. But suddenly it felt as though seeing him had become a need—almost as much as the air she breathed. When had such a shift occurred?

"May I escort you back to the house? I should not like you to slip on the ice again."

Gabby smiled up at him. "It seems you already are." She motioned to the corner of the house they had just reached. "Although I do not believe there is reason for concern. I am rather sure-footed when I do not have a kitten underfoot." She patted Sophia lightly on the head.

Aaron reached out, and in one fluid motion swung Sophia up, settling her in his arms. "I can't risk having her trip you up again."

Sophia whimpered until Gabby reached out, gently squeezing the girl's hand. "Do not be frightened, Soph. Lord Brinton will not harm you."

Sophia put her wet mittened hands on his cheeks and studied Aaron's face. Apparently, she approved of what she saw because she settled against his chest as they rounded the corner.

"Thank you. She is tired and was walking slower with every step." Even as she said the words her stomach hardened. Had he not wrapped her in those arms only moments ago? Gabby longed to be there again, but Sophia had that pleasure now.

"I am happy to be of service." Aaron's strides were at least twice as long as hers, and she had to skip to keep up.

By the time they arrived at the front stairs, she felt as though *she* may need a nap. They mounted the stairs, and Aaron pushed the door open, stepping to the side to allow her to enter first.

Gabby paused inside the door, only then realizing just how cold she was. The footman stepped from the cloakroom and waited patiently at her elbow. She unfastened her pelisse and handed it over with her bonnet and gloves. Her fingers ached with cold.

She felt Aaron beside her before she looked up into his face. He nodded to the little girl in his arms. "It seems she has grown accustomed to me."

Gabby went up on tiptoes, peering over his arms.

Sophia's lashes rested against her cheeks, and her lips parted slightly. She took in a deep breath but relaxed again against Aaron's chest.

"Oh, dear. She will be unhappy she succumbed." Gabby dropped onto her heels. "Let me take her up to the nursery."

He shook his head. "Let me. She is much too heavy for you to carry her so far." He started for the stairs.

She reached out her hand and stopped him. "But you have not yet removed your coat. Give her to me and I will settle her into bed."

He shook his head. "I insist on taking her." A thought flitted through Gabby's mind. Is this how Aaron would be with his own children? It wasn't hard for her to picture it.

"Now please, lead the way, Gabby."

Her heart gave a lurch. He had called her Gabby.

She'd wanted to give him leave to use her father's pet name for her but had worried he would think her too improper. She had seen what he'd thought of Rebekah when she had acted in such a manner.

"Gabby. While I enjoy standing here watching you think, Sophia is only becoming heavier."

"Oh. I'm sorry." She hurried past him and up the stairs.

She twisted the knob and pushed the nursery door open. Nurse Jones sat in the rocking chair by the fire, mending in her lap. She looked up at the sound of the door and offered Gabby a smile. "I am surprised she lasted this long."

Gabby motioned to Aaron as he walked through the door. "She didn't."

Nurse Jones chuckled. Placing her hands on the arms of the rocker, she let out a groan.

Gabby held up her hand. "Please, do not get up. We can see she is settled."

Nurse Jones sighed but settled back into the rocker. "Thank you. These old bones just don't move as quickly as they once did."

Aaron followed Gabby into the nursery. The curtains were partially drawn, casting the room in shadows.

She pointed to a bed. "Just lay her there and I will remove her coat."

Aaron gently set her on the bed and took a step back. He stood with his hands at his side, watching over her shoulder as Gabby pulled Sophia's arms out of the sleeves. She looked up at him. "You are wet through yourself. Thank you for your help, but I can see to her now."

His brow furrowed, and he looked down at his wet greatcoat. "I suppose you're right. If you're certain you no longer have need of my assistance..." He seemed hesitant to leave, and Gabby was equally reluctant to have him go.

"I shall take my coat downstairs," he said, even though he remained firmly rooted in place. He looked around them. "But then I believe I shall spend the rest of the afternoon in the library." He placed an emphasis on the last words. But that was silly. Why would he do that?

Gabby smiled up at him.

His face held a soft smile as he watched her.

Gabby felt her own face warm. While there was nothing indecent happening, the moment felt intimate. What would it be like to share a home and have children with this man? Her cheeks flamed. That thought was certainly indecent. She placed her hand to her cheek, grateful for the dimness that surrounded them.

She turned her attention back to Sophia, smoothing her hair away from her face.

"It has been a good day."

Gabby barely heard Aaron's whispered voice. Had he sensed her thoughts? Perhaps the low light in the room had not hidden the blush in her cheeks as well as she thought.

Gabby turned to acknowledge him, but all she saw was his back as he slipped through the door.

The room felt colder and darker with him gone.

Sophia sighed and Gabby pulled the bedsheet and counterpane up over the girl's small body.

Gabby's eyes felt heavy. Maybe she should crawl in and rest with Sophia. A deep voice floated through her mind. *I believe I shall spend the rest of the afternoon in the library.* Yes, the library *did* seem a good place to spend the afternoon.

She stoked the fire and slipped out of the room.

Nurse Jones looked up. "I shall sit with her. Thank you for seeing to her."

"You're welcome. You know I enjoy spending time with her."

Nurse Jones gingerly stood up and moved toward the nursery door. "She loves you. Now go enjoy your afternoon. I thought I heard Lord Brinton say he would be in the library." The older woman smiled knowingly.

Gabby bit the inside of her cheek, suddenly self-conscious. Had she made Nurse Jones believe she had feelings for Aaron? It was true; she had such feelings. But it was not something she wished for the whole house to know. "Yes, I recall him saying that as well. But I do not believe he was desiring company." She turned to leave. "I will be in my chambers if you should need me."

Her shoulders sagged. She had been looking forward to seeing Aaron in the library. But she could not very well go there now. It would only confirm what surely everyone in the house was thinking—that Gabby had designs on Lord Brinton.

She plodded down the stairs and headed toward her room, pausing at the door to the upper floor of the library. She stared at the door. Should she go in? It was not as if Nurse Jones would come looking for her and confirm her suspicions.

But what if something happened, and she *did* come looking? Gabby sighed. That had only occurred a handful of times. It seemed unlikely that it should happen today. Her heart thudded in her chest. Aaron had probably not even arrived yet. She could just slip in, grab a few books, and return to her room to read, just as she had said she would do.

She reached for the knob but pulled her hand back. What if he *was* inside? Had he mentioned the library so she would come and join him? Or was he giving her notice that he would occupy the library and did not wish for company? He knew she frequented the library, so it was feasible he was just informing her of his desire to be alone.

Zut! She seemed incapable of making even the smallest decision.

She shook her head firmly and pushed open the door. She would retrieve her books and leave. If Aaron was inside, she would just walk quietly so as not to disturb him.

She stepped inside and turned to close the door behind her.

"I'm glad you decided to join me. I confess, I was doubting if you would."

Her hand stilled on the knob; her heart thundered in her ears. He *had* wanted her to come? "I had thought to retrieve my books so as not to disturb you." She turned around, resting her back against the door.

She could just see the top of his soft-looking hair where he sat on the settee below by the fire. There was no way he could have seen her. How had he known it was her?

"You are not disturbing me."

She heard him close a book and set it on a table. A quiet rustling drifted up and a moment later, he stepped onto the second floor. It reminded her of the first time she'd come to this room and he had discovered her. Although, she did not remember there being a whooshing in her ears or a weakness in her knees. She pressed herself tighter against the door.

These feelings confused her and she did not know what to do with them. She could not say for certain she even knew what they meant. No one had ever told her what it felt like to be in love. Perhaps this was something different.

He stopped several feet away from her. "It is cool up here. Are you sure you would not be more comfortable down by the fire?" He shifted from one foot to the other, studying her. A grunt sounded deep in his throat. "Perhaps it is *I* who am bothering you." His brow creased, and he took a step back.

"No." Gabby's voice came out much louder than she'd intended. "I see no reason we cannot both enjoy the room." She pulled her bottom lip between her teeth and his gaze dropped to her mouth.

His eyes shone, and his lips parted slightly. It was the same look he'd given her when they had fallen in the snow. He shook his head and clasped his hands together. "Uh, yes. That would..." His eyes dropped to her lips again. "What I mean to say is, uh, I would enjoy it —you being here too." He sucked in a deep sigh and scowled in obvious frustration.

Gabby stepped toward him and reached out, pressing her hand to his forearm. "I would enjoy it as well."

His throat bobbed up and down, but his posture relaxed. "It is settled then. We shall read together."

CHAPTER 16

Aaron walked down the corridor with Kirtley at his side. They had cut their evening port short so they could join the ladies in the drawing room. The ladies. Lady was perhaps a better term where Aaron was concerned as there was only one he cared to see tonight.

He'd thought of hardly anything else the whole of the day. And yesterday. And even the day before. He thought on her almost to the point of distraction. There had been several times when he was speaking to someone and they had to repeat themselves because Aaron had not been listening the first time.

He shook his head. What was wrong with him? How had he let her invade his thoughts so thoroughly?

It had started the other day with the snowball fight and their near kiss—no, it had started even before that. Had he not been waiting for her in the library for hours? *Oh, the library.* How had he thought them being together there—together—a good idea?

He had enjoyed her company. Just having her close to him was better than he could imagine. That was not the problem. The notion that it took all of his restraint not to lean over and kiss her was the problem. And not just once, but repeatedly. It was a blessing the door was open, and a maid present.

Even still, Aaron had studied her lips so intently, he felt he already knew them quite intimately.

He pulled at his collar. How could he be such a rake?

Gabby was a lady and deserved admiration, not ogling.

Kirtley cleared his throat. "Are you listening to a word I've said?"

Aaron stared at him. "What?" Lud, he had done it again.

Kirtley threw his head back and laughed. "You have been wool-gathering the whole evening. Tell me, what has you so captivated?" His eyes sparkled and Aaron could tell he was holding back more laughter.

Aaron reached out a hand and pulled Kirtley to a stop, even though a part of him wanted to punch his friend in the mouth, but more pressing matters took precedence. "You love Lady Kirtley, do you not?"

Kirtley raised a brow but nodded. "Very much. But you knew that already."

"Yes. As I mentioned before, it is obvious in the way you look on her—as if there is nothing else in the world but her." Aaron's mouth twisted. How much did he confide in his friend? "Was it always such?"

Kirtley folded his arms across his chest? "Do you mean to ask if I always looked on her in that way?"

Aaron nodded.

"I like to believe I hid my emotions until I was certain of hers. You see, I fell in love with Eleanor almost the moment I saw her. But Eleanor will tell you I failed quite miserably in my disguise." He grinned. "She will also suggest it took her a bit more time to discover she loved me also." Kirtley nudged Aaron. "But it is all a Banbury story."

"How did you know? That it was love, I mean. I have never considered myself in love before."

"But you consider yourself in love now?"

Aaron shrugged. "I cannot say for sure. I am not certain I would know it when it happens."

Kirtley cleared his throat. "*When* it happens?"

Aaron's cravat felt constrictive on his neck and he pulled it away from his skin. Why had he thought to have this conversation with Kirtley? Surely this was a conversation to have with...who? Not his mother, that was for certain. That would be a disaster. And while he was beginning to feel that he could talk to Gabby about most things, *this* was not one of them. Lud. Why had he not just figured it out on his own?

Kirtley nodded. He knew Aaron was not being entirely truthful. But was Aaron really lying?

His head told him he was not in love with Gabby, that it was merely desire for a beautiful woman, though that thought made him want to land himself a facer. But his heart was not so easily deterred. It hammered and skittered and tightened, sometimes all at the same time, when Gabby was around. Or when he thought on her. Or smelled something that reminded him of her.

Gah. He was an idiot. But the whole thing left him feeling slightly confused about which organ he should believe. Head or heart?

"You are only fooling yourself, you know." Kirtley leaned back against the wall. "I believe everyone in the house but you knows you are in love."

Aaron narrowed his eyes. "Oh? And what gives you that notion?"

"Come, man. For the same reason you knew of my feelings for Eleanor. It is written upon your face whenever you see *her*."

Aaron sighed again. "You never answered my question. How did you know?"

Kirtley stared at him. "When did I know? I knew when she would not leave my thoughts or my dreams. When I made up excuses to see her just so I could be in the same room with her. I knew when everything I saw brought her face to my mind. When I could not imagine living without her at my side. And a dozen other reasons."

Aaron rubbed at his neck. Kirtley had almost completely described his own feelings for Gabby. Did that mean his heart was correct?

"But she is French. That changes things." But did it really? Or was he just using it as an excuse. And why was he looking for excuses?

Kirtley tsked. "There will not always be a war, Brinton. Besides, she is sounding less and less French every day. I say the devil take hindmost. If you love her, do not wait for the Season. There are many who will not care a wit about her nationality when they discover the amount of her dowry."

Aaron frowned. "I don't care about her dowry."

Kirtley nodded, continuing to grin. "Yes, I know."

They continued down the corridor.

If everyone knew Aaron loved her, did that mean Gabby did also? Whether she did or did not, how did he proceed? He had been so horrible to her in the beginning. How did one even begin to make amends for that?

He shook his head. "Then it seems even more cruel that she will never accept me."

"Gabby? Never accept you? You are dafter than I thought." Kirtley thumped Aaron on the back and laughed. When had his laugh become so annoying? "It is not Gabby you will have to convince—she is yours and has been for some time, I believe."

Aaron's brow crinkled. "Then whom shall I need to convince?"

Kirtley laughed again. "Peter. Lord Rockwell is very protective of his ward, every bit as much as a brother would be." Kirtley thumped him one more time. "I would not buy the special license just yet."

Rockwell?

Aaron had forgotten about him. They were friends. But why should Kirtley think Rockwell would disapprove of Aaron? That was something new he needed to ponder. Later.

They stepped into the drawing room, and Aaron's gaze immediately swept the group, stopping only when he spotted her.

She sat on the settee at the far side of the room, her head bent toward Rebekah as the two talked. Gabby smiled and laughed quietly, touching Rebekah on the arm.

Aaron stood just inside the door, in no hurry to join the conversations buzzing about. "As I said, I should not think she will stay a *miss* long once the Season is underway. I would not delay if I were you."

Even the thought of someone else making an offer for Gabby made Aaron's throat tighten. He swallowed painfully.

Could Kirtley be correct? Had Gabby already forgiven him?

Kirtley moved away, leaving Aaron to watch Gabby alone for a moment longer. He knew he needed to join the group eventually, but for now, he was content. It was as if, for this one instant, his life was very nearly perfect.

As if sensing his gaze, Gabby looked back over her shoulder toward the doorway, her lips curving until the whole of her face smiled.

Aaron's chest squeezed. Was this feeling one of the indicators Kirtley had used? If not, he should add it to the list.

Aaron made his way over to the group clustered around the fire, his gaze never leaving Gabby.

His mother looked up at his approach. Her brow creased, and she flicked a glance to Gabby, before giving a smile. "Aaron, dearest. I am glad you did not linger over your port this evening."

He found it hard to pull his gaze away, but he did it anyway. "Oh, and why is that, Mother?"

"I should like to play a game. We have played none of the games we usually play at Christmastide. If Hen—" She halted. "That is to say, I thought it could be fun."

Aaron stared at his mother, but she ducked her head. "I could not agree more, Mother. What shall we play?"

She lifted her head and her eyes brightened as if she had thought he would refuse her. "What about a game of move-all?"

Rebekah clapped her hands. "I adore that game. It is part of my family's Christmastide tradition. I admit to feeling a bit out of sorts over missing out this year."

"Gather the chairs around in a circle then." Aaron nearly laughed out loud. This was a perfect game. If he was lucky, he may just get Gabby—if not on top of him like she had been in the snow—at least on his lap for a moment. And he could not think of anything better. It would be less obvious what he was trying to do if there were more people here to play, but there were not. He would just need to be sneakier in his attempts. Might they even hold hands?

"What do you think about asking Miss Carter to join us?" Gabby asked.

Had she read his mind? Although only one additional person was not the crowds of people he'd hoped could distract from his ulterior motives.

Lady Kirtley nodded. "I see no reason for her not to join us. Nurse Jones can look after the children for the evening."

"I shall fetch her then." Gabby stood.

"Wait." Aaron nearly lunged to stop her. If Gabby went to the nursery, it might be hours before she returned—if she returned at all. And that did not fit into his plans for the evening. "I shall send a maid to fetch her."

Gabby raised a brow. "That is unnecessary. You need not trouble a maid."

Aaron dashed to the bell pull. "Come now. We both know if Miss Sophia sees you in the nursery, she will not allow you to leave."

Lady Kirtley nodded. "He is correct, Gabby. She was asking for you before supper."

"She was?"

Lady Kirtley held up a hand. "You are not going to her. I am certain she is asleep by now. You may see her in the morning."

Gabby smiled mischievously. "But if Sophia is already asleep, why can I not go fetch Miss Carter?"

Lady Kirtley shook her head in vexation.

"You rang, my lord." A maid dipped a curtsy at the doorway.

"Thank the heavens your staff is prompt, my lord." Lady Kirtley cast a look at Gabby.

"Yes, Lucy. Please have Miss Carter fetched from the school-room. We should like another person to play move-all with us."

The maid curtsied and disappeared as they pushed a table against the wall, making room for six chairs. They spaced them evenly in a circle and then waited for Miss Carter to arrive.

Aaron moved in next to Gabby. He leaned down close to her ear. "Tell me, Gabby," he whispered. "Have you ever played move-all before?"

She held still, but he observed the gooseflesh dotting her skin between the tops of her long gloves and the bottom of her sleeve. He thrilled at the knowledge that he could affect her so. Perhaps Kirtley was right, and Aaron need only worry about Rockwell.

She shook her head. "No. I was hoping someone might explain it to me before we start."

"Let me do the honors." He took the chance to move even closer, the folds of her skirt rubbing against his leg. He pointed to the circle. "One person will stand in the middle while everyone else takes a seat. The person in the middle hollers 'move all' and everyone must find a different chair. The person left without a seat becomes the new caller in the center and the game begins again."

Gabby nodded. "That does not seem too complicated."

Aaron nodded. "I believe it shall be rather fun." *He* intended to have a great deal of fun, anyhow. He could already picture her face as he slid into a chair just before her. He grinned and glanced up as Rebekah moved into his line of sight. "Oh, Gabby, I have been meaning to thank you."

She turned her head toward him, and their noses nearly touched. She pulled back slightly. "Me? But why? What do you have to thank me for?"

He motioned with his head to Rebekah. "Rebekah told me of her decision. She mentioned you were very helpful in making it."

Gabby grunted and shrugged. "I believe she is giving me undue credit. My only advice was that we both needed to accept our fates and move on with our lives as quickly as possible."

Accept their fates? What fate did Gabby think she had? Surely if she had an arrangement with someone else, Kirtley would have mentioned it. "Yes, well, whatever you said, it seemed to be of help to her."

"I am glad for it. She has become a dear friend and I should like to see her happily settled."

"I am grateful for your friendship toward her. She has not seemed as sad of late. I am certain that is, in part, thanks to you."

Gabby shook her head but was kept from a reply when Miss Carter stepped into the room. "You asked to see me, my lady?" She looked concerned, as if she feared she may be in trouble.

"Yes, Miss Carter. Miss Babineaux thought you might enjoy playing some games with us this evening."

Miss Carter flicked her gaze to Gabby, before returning it to Lady Kirtley. Her brow creased, and she twisted her hands. "I would enjoy playing. Thank you for thinking of me, my lady." Aaron noted the governess thanked Lady Kirtley, rather than Gabby, even though Gabby was the one who had suggested she be included. This was not the first time he had sensed tension between the two women.

"Let us begin the game." His mother waved everyone to the circle. "I was the one to suggest the game, so I believe it only proper that I shall start in the middle."

"Oh no, my lady. I would be happy to start in the middle." Rebekah shooed the dowager viscountess to a chair. "It is just as we played it when I was a girl. I always started the game off."

Aaron lifted his elbow to Gabby. "May I escort you to the circle, Miss Babineaux?"

She chuckled but placed her hand on his arm.

It may have only been for four steps, but it was worth it. Aaron realized that he had been wrong earlier. *This* was the moment that his life was nearly perfect. He glanced over at Gabby and there was only one thing that could make it even more so. He just needed to plan the best time to speak to her about it.

They moved into the circle. The only chairs not taken were across from each other.

Aaron led Gabby to one of them. "I hope this one will suffice."

She dipped her head. "Of course, my lord. Thank you."

Everyone sat, leaning slightly forward in anticipation of the call. Rebekah turned in a slow circle, eyeing each person as she turned. "Move all!" she yelled, and everyone clamored from their seats.

Aaron kept his eyes on Gabby, looking for which direction she would go. She raced toward the seat next to him.

He waited a second and sat in the chair. But he had timed it too late, meaning he was the one on Gabby's lap.

A low roar of laughter sounded when everyone noticed their predicament.

Gabby let out a squeak, and he looked over his shoulder to see her face a pretty shade of pink. It was not as he had planned, but it was not in the least bit unpleasant.

Still, it meant *he* was in the center for this round—not that that would change his plans any.

He replaced Rebekah, turning around and around. He kept his eyes on Gabby and hollered "move all," this time making sure he made it to the chair first.

She slid onto his lap, the fabric of her skirt slipping beneath her and nearly sending her to the ground.

He grinned as he wrapped his arms around her waist. "Woah. Don't slide onto the floor." He doubted most of the others would believe Gabby's rescue was his only motivation. From the double brow raise from Kirtley, Aaron knew he'd not fooled his friend. But he did not care in the least. Gabby was in his arms, even if it was only for a moment.

"It seems I am the one in the middle this time," she said.

He sighed and gave her a slight squeeze—one he hoped no one else noticed—just before releasing her to stand. When she didn't stand immediately, he thought to pull her back to him but did not act fast enough before she stood, moving to the center.

She turned in a circle and he watched her eyes, looking for where she would run next.

Kirtley nodded to him, and Aaron knew he had an ally.

"Move all," Gabby yelled and raced to a chair opposite of where Aaron had been seated.

Aaron hurried over, but found he was not the only one vying for the spot. Miss Carter, a stouter lady than Gabby, was there also. She moved toward the chair, giving a flick of her hips as she sat and sending Gabby sprawling to the floor.

Gabby landed hard on the rug. "Ooh."

Aaron reached down to help her up. "Are you alright?" What was Miss Carter about? He knew she was not fond of Gabby, but this seemed wholly out of line.

Gabby stood up, rubbing at her elbow that had obviously hit one of the chairs on her way down. She looked over at Miss Carter who looked up with doe eyed innocence. "Pardon me, Miss Babineaux. Are you well?"

Gabby smiled tightly and Aaron had the urge to call the governess out.

"Quite well, thank you." Gabby stepped back to the middle of the circle. "I suppose I am it again."

Aaron moved up beside her. "I will take this turn." He scowled at Miss Carter over his shoulder.

"No. I did not secure a seat. I shall take my turn like everyone else." Gabby shooed him toward the seat. Which he had never actually sat in, so Gabby could sit there and still be within the rules of the game.

But Aaron had a feeling she would not welcome this suggestion. Instead he sat down and waited for her to begin again. But his objectives had changed—or rather been added to. Now he would not only be trying to get Gabby to sit on his lap but protect her from Miss Carter in the process.

CHAPTER 17

Gabby stood in front of the mirror, turning this way and that. A large purple bruise covered her elbow and she knew several more colored her hips and thighs. The previous evenings *fun* and games had turned rather brutal rather quickly. More than once, Gabby had found herself deposited on the floor while Miss Carter looked smugly down at her.

But the occasions when Gabby had sent Miss Carter to the floor, were no less bruising and painful, though they did hold a certain degree of satisfaction. Still, Gabby felt every painful swish of her dress and breath that she took. Perhaps they should have played the *move-all* game earlier in Christmastide Season so as not to have these bruises for the ball tonight. It had convinced her that nothing she said to Miss Carter would make a difference. The woman was determined to hate Gabby.

Gabby ran her hands down the front of her gown. Even with the bruises, she felt pretty in it. The pale green gown with a golden lace overdress brightened her eyes, bringing out the honey-colored flecks. It was one reason Eleanor had insisted they buy it before leaving London. Gabby had intended to keep it tucked away until they returned for the Season. It was just the kind of gown to make an impression at one of the more fashionable society balls. And she needed to make an impression, just not in London as she had previously thought.

She glanced out the darkened window. The weather had remained clear for the past few days, and it had looked as if they may return to London, rather than moving on to Dovehaven after tonight's Twelfth Night ball.

Tonight was the reason Gabby had brought this dress with her, rather than leaving it at Penderton House. She lifted the overlay away from the underdress and twisted from side to side. This would do nicely.

Aaron had looked at her differently over the last few days. It was foolish to hope, but she couldn't help it. And tonight, she wanted to feel special—to feel beautiful.

She swallowed.

But would Aaron agree? He often made up excuses to seek her out and spend time with her. She could almost guarantee if she went to the library, he would appear before too long. That did not mean he loved her, but it meant something, did it not?

Gabby put a hand to her stomach and sucked in a breath.

She blinked rapidly several times and shook her head. She was being silly. How could someone like Aaron possibly love someone like her? She did not come from the *Beau monde.* And while she may have had aristocratic grandparents, she had not even known them—something obviously not in her favor.

It was possible she had conjured this supposed attraction in her mind. She'd heard of it happening before—someone wanting something so badly they saw things that were not really there.

She took in a calming breath.

"What ees zee matter? Vous look lovely zis evening." Aline looked over Gabby's shoulder and stared into the mirror.

"Nothing is amiss. I am just nervous. What if no one asks me to dance? We have seen how people react when they realize I am French."

Aline smiled and patted Gabby's arm. "You are much too beautiful for gentlemen to ignore you for long. Besides, once zey learn of your goodness, zey will forget all about your nationality."

Gabby smiled half-heartedly. "Thank you, Aline."

Aline gave Gabby's shoulders a squeeze. Her maid had only meant to encourage and reassure, but it saddened Gabby.

She missed having a mother to guide and encourage her. She hardly remembered her, recalling only snippets of memories. And while her father had been attentive, it was not the same.

She blinked back the tears pooling in the bottoms of her lids. Now was not the time to become a watering pot. She'd known girls in France whose mothers were kind and caring. But she'd also known many whose mothers were anything but loving. So perhaps she was just as well with Aline.

Gabby turned and hugged her maid. "Thank you."

The woman stiffened at first, but then relaxed and hugged Gabby back. "You're welcome, miss."

A knock sounded and Aline moved to answer it, but Eleanor pushed into the room before Aline had a chance to open it.

"Gabby?" Eleanor nearly floated into the room.

"Eleanor, you look lovely this evening."

Eleanor smiled. "Thank you." She stood back and looked Gabby over from head to toe.

Gabby's hands shook. Would she approve of what she saw?

"Oh, this gown is everything I thought it would be." She placed her finger to her lips. "But something is missing..."

Gabby turned and looked into the mirror. She twisted her head to one side then the other. Had she missed something earlier? There did not appear to be anything wrong with the back. Her hand flew to her hair. Perhaps that is where the problem lay. Her fingertips gently caressed the tiny pearls Aline had woven into the plaits and knot.

"I do not understand—"

A string of golden pearls swung over her head and rested against her collarbone. Eleanor fastened the necklace and stepped back. "Now you are ready."

The pearls felt cool on her skin, but Gabby could not pull her gaze away from how they looked around her neck. "I cannot take your pearls, Eleanor."

Eleanor smiled. "They are not my pearls, Gabby. They are yours."

Gabby shook her head. "No, they are not."

"They belonged to your mother. Your father's solicitor sent them to Peter, along with a few other items your father wished for you to have. Peter delivered them just before we left London. He wanted you to have them for the upcoming Season. I had planned to leave them at Penderton House, but at the last minute I brought them with us." She sighed. "I am so glad that I did."

How had she never seen them before? Had Peter really purchased them and used her mother as an excuse? "But I have never seen them before—never been told about them."

Eleanor shrugged gracefully—something Gabby knew she could never accomplish. "I am in earnest, Gabby."

"It is not you I am questioning, Eleanor." Gabby pulled her long gloves off the table and pulled them on one by one. She turned back toward the mirror and grunted, running her fingers over the pearls one more time. Had these really been her mother's? Had Eleanor sensed Gabby's need for a connection to her mother? Is that why she had brought the necklace?

Whatever it was, Gabby was grateful, even if the necklace did not make her any less nervous. The longer she stared in the mirror, the more her anxiety grew. "We should be going. I'm certain Lord and Lady Brinton are downstairs waiting."

She swallowed hard again. The time had come. She placed a smile on her face and pretended that all was well, as opposed to how she really felt—as if a den of fox cubs rolled around in her stomach.

Gabby and Eleanor sauntered down the corridor. "Gabby, relax."

Gabby looked over at Eleanor. "What if no one dances with me?"

Eleanor smiled. "I am certain you will dance with at least one gentleman. And others will follow." She patted Gabby on the arm. "Hugh will dance with you also. So you are certain of two sets, at least."

Gabby smirked. "Two sets? That is all I am assured? That is dismal, indeed."

Eleanor nodded. "That is more like it. That is the Gabby that has won Lord Brinton's heart."

Gabby stopped at the top of the stairs. "Do you really think so?"

"I am certain he will offer for you before the Season is underway. I shall be surprised if he does not do so before we depart." Eleanor squared her shoulders. "Now, it looks as if they are waiting for us."

They moved down the first set of stairs. Aaron was the first to capture her attention. He stood in the entryway looking more handsome than any gentleman ought in his black superfine tailcoat. The dowager viscountess stood at his side and Rebekah next to her.

Aaron greeted Eleanor first with a smile, but Gabby could see it was only superficial; the twinkle she'd recently seen in his eyes was absent.

Or it was until his gaze found her as she stepped onto the marble-tiled floor.

Her breath hitched.

He stopped mid-conversation, his face relaxing into an affable grin. The dimple at the side of his eye, the one that only came out when he was genuinely smiling, appeared.

There it was. The look that gave her hope he felt for her the same way she felt for him. He stepped forward and bowed. "Good evening, Miss Babineaux." His eyes never left her face, even as he bent low.

Gabby curtsied. "My lord. Thank you for the invitation. It was very kind of you." What was she babbling about?

Lady Kirtley sidled up to Gabby's side. "Guests will arrive at any moment. Perhaps we should allow Lord Brinton to prepare for the evening."

"I believe everything is ready. However, there was a chalk picture in the ballroom I wished to show Miss Babineaux before it becomes smudged." Aaron stepped away from his mother and Rebekah. "If you will excuse us." He cupped Gabby's elbow and guided her away from the receiving line. "I regret my guests will require my attention for some time. It will be dull, to be sure. But I had hoped to claim your supper dance."

"I will save it for you." Gabby raised her hand to the pearls around her neck, only then noticing her pulse that was surely about to burst through her skin. She glanced behind her as they passed through the ballroom doors. Her face warmed when she caught sight of Lord Kirtley's raised brows and approving smile.

Aaron removed his hand from her elbow, instead, tucking her hand in the crook of his elbow. "Miss Babineaux, you will be quite sought after this evening, of that, I have no doubt." That brought a frown to his face. "I am happy to have these few moments with you before the guests arrive."

They stopped at the edge of the ballroom floor. Chalk created intricate patterns of vines, flowers, and leaves on the floor around the perimeter of the room. The center held a large design of a mariner's compass in differing hues of grays and blacks.

Half a dozen golden chandeliers glittered in the candlelight, shadows dancing on the floor, even though the orchestra had not yet played their first notes.

"It is beautiful," Gabby whispered in an awestruck voice. She dropped her hand from his arm and tilted her head back, taking in the fresco and the coffered ceilings.

"I am glad you approve." His voice tickled the space between her earlobe and her collarbone at the same time his hand rested at the small of her back. Suddenly, just breathing took all of her concentration.

They circled the room—Aaron intent on the artwork of both the ceiling and the floor.

His hand dropped away from her back, the heat noticeably

absent. But before she could lament its departure too much, he captured her hand in his. She could not decide which she liked better.

He pointed out distinct elements of the art, but Gabby paid minimal attention to his words.

Breathing still felt deliberate and her hand felt warm and tingly in his. Everything seemed right in this moment, and she wished it would never end.

They reached the far end of the room, and Aaron pulled her to a stop.

She looked up into his face. Why had they stopped? Had he realized she paid no attention to anything he said? Or was there something here he wished to point out?

He moved in front of her, staring down at her with an intensity in his gaze she was coming to recognize.

Her heart skittered in her chest. Was this it? Was this when he was going to tell her he loved her?

He flicked his eyes upward. His brows rose and he tilted his head slightly to the side, a crooked grin on his lips.

Gabby followed his gaze and her mouth fell open.

He *had* stopped her for a reason—wished for her to notice something.

A kissing ball hung just above their heads. They had been hanging about the house for more than a week but never had she stopped beneath one. That was not to say she had not imagined what could happen if she were to stop. She had imagined it. Many times over.

Gabby bit her lower lip, releasing it when Lady Kirtley's warnings sounded in her head. Now was not the time for dried, cracked lips.

They stood for a moment, both looking questioningly at each other. Did he want her to kiss him? Gabby's heart gave a painful thump. She did not think she could do it. But she did not need to question for long.

His head lowered slowly, giving her a chance to move away if she desired.

But she didn't desire it. She was almost embarrassed to admit to herself what she wanted. Her muscles jumped in anticipation, her pulse hammering in her ears and neck.

He released her hand and ran his fingers lightly up her arm, resting his hand just below her earlobe. He grinned, obviously feeling the thumping beneath his fingertips. Taking it as permission, he closed the distance and covered her lips with his.

Gabby let out a whimper. She had never seen fireworks—only heard about them. Her father had told her a person could feel the power and energy of the explosion. But she'd never understood his meaning until now. She was certain they could not be half so spectacular or powerful as the energy pulsing through her body. It was frightening and exhilarating.

She raised her hands to his chest, grasping the lapels of his coat, both to keep herself standing and to bring him closer.

He sighed and deepened the kiss, sliding his other hand around her waist to the small of her back.

Hand holding was delightful, but his hand on her back was undoubtedly her favorite. She yielded willingly, allowing him to tighten his hold and pull her closer to him. "Gabby," he mumbled against her lips. "I want to ask—"

A gasp pierced the air, and Gabby released his coat, pushing away from him. Lord and Lady Kirtley stood in the doorway. Eleanor's hands flapped at her side, like a baby bird trying to fly, her mouth and eyes gaping open. The overall effect was less than flattering.

Lord Kirtley, however, grinned broadly, his head nodding with approval.

"What are you doing?" Lady Kirtley shrieked as she took three long steps toward them, her glare searing into Aaron.

"I believe you know what they were doing, my love." Kirtley walked beside his wife with far less purpose in his stride.

She shot him a withering glance before turning it on Aaron. "I knew you favored her, but my lord! But...are you trying to ruin her?"

"No, surely not." Aaron stepped slightly behind Gabby. Was he seeking shelter from Eleanor? Her back stiffened until he unclasped his hands to take hold of hers. "I am sorry, Gabby. That was not completely my intent in bringing you in here." His voice was a pained whisper.

Gabby realized she had been too hasty earlier in declaring his hand on her back the decided winner. Because, now, the feel of her hand in his was amazing. It gave her confidence and reassurance. Both of which she needed to face Eleanor.

"What have we done wrong?" His voice was stronger than it had been when he apologized. "Are we not standing under a kissing ball? What is it for if not kissing? It would have been an unpardonable offense to the lady had I not done as tradition holds." He squeezed her hand and stepped up closer behind her.

Lady Kirtley huffed. "A kiss on the cheek is acceptable, perhaps even a quick kiss on the lips. But that...that was not just a kiss. That was..." Her head shook as she sputtered. "Well, I am not going to voice what *that* was. No proper lady would." She turned to her husband for support, but he only shrugged. "Are you not to do anything, Hugh? Will you allow him to take such liberties with Gabby?"

"Aside from asking for pointers, I should think not." He slid a hand around his wife's waist and led her off to the side. "They are in love, Eleanor, as you are aware. No one else saw them. I do not see any reason to do anything other than pat Lord Brinton on the back."

She opened and shut her mouth several times, but he stopped her.

"Let it happen naturally, Ellie. Brinton could not kiss a lady in such a manner, and not have plans to marry her. Let it be for now. If, when the Season begins, he has not offered for her, *then* I shall call him out."

Gabby's face burned with humiliation at every sentence Lord

Kirtley spoke. For her part, Gabby knew Lord Kirtley was right. She *did* love Lord Brinton. But what of him? Was Eleanor right? What were his intentions?

She ran the back of her hand over her pulsating lips. Could he kiss her like that if he did not love her as Lord Kirtley had insinuated? There were men who could, Gabby knew. But was Aaron such a man? If he was, would he not have given in to Lady Brinton's advances?

Lady Kirtley broke away from her husband's side and came to Gabby. "Come, Gabrielle, let us fix you up before anyone can see what he has done." She cast another withering glare at Aaron.

Aaron lifted a hand. "But I have not finished—"

Eleanor glared over her shoulder. "You most certainly have finished, my lord."

His head shook and he muttered to himself. He was no doubt regretting his actions.

Tears gathered in Gabby's eyes, but she did not know if they were due to Eleanor's reprimand or her embarrassment at being caught so thoroughly kissing Lord Brinton. Or it could simply be because the most enjoyable moment of her life had come to such an abrupt end. Whatever it was, she knew she should have felt a sting of regret, but she did not. Rather, she wished for a quiet corner where the kiss could happen again and again.

Lord Kirtley moved in next to Aaron. "Carriages are arriving. I should guess your first guest will be inside shortly."

"Gabby?" Aaron's voice was strained.

She stopped and looked over her shoulder at him.

"Don't forget you promised me the supper dance."

She sighed and nodded. "I will not." Unless of course, Eleanor locked her away so as to keep any more kisses from happening.

They cleared the doorway before Eleanor turned and whispered in her ear. "What did you think you were doing in there? What if it had been a guest who happened upon you? Do you not understand the repercussions?"

Gabby pulled up. "Eleanor, I thought you of all people would understand. I know you love Lord Kirtley. I see the way you look at each other. Have you never kissed him in the same way I kissed Lord Brinton?"

Her face pinked. "My kissing Lord Kirtley is not what we are discussing." Lady Kirtley stared hard at Gabby. "You *do* love him, then?"

Gabby nodded.

"I knew it." She sounded superior. Air pushed from her lungs. "No more kissing until banns have been posted, do you understand?"

As much as she regretted the notion, Gabby nodded. "The kissing balls will be burned tonight, will they not?"

Eleanor sighed. "Fortunately, yes. Now if we can keep you out from under them until then, perhaps your reputation will stay intact," Eleanor grumbled.

CHAPTER 18

Gabby did not know a dance could be so thrilling, so wistful, so...wonderful. At least, not until Aaron had led her out onto the floor.

She had danced every set before the supper dance. Her partners, for the most part, were adequate dancers and amiable partners.

Aaron had been absent for the first several sets. But once he'd come into the ballroom, she had watched him from beneath her lashes as he danced with other ladies. She tried to school her features but did not feel very successful at the task, scowling at many young ladies as they twirled about in his arms.

He smiled and made conversation, but she was pleased to note that his dimple never made an appearance—not until he looked down the line and caught her eye.

And then he stood before her, bowed low. "Miss Babineaux, I believe I claimed this dance."

She'd nodded, unable to hide her happiness. "Yes, I believe you did." She had wondered if he would come to regret their kiss once he'd had a chance to think on it. But if he had, would he be this eager to dance with her?

He placed her hand on his arm and led her out to the dance floor. The music played, and he bowed to her as she curtsied. They clasped hands, and it felt nothing like the other partners she had danced with. He brought her toward him and then backed away. She thrilled at the warmth of her hand in his. But then he dropped it and she moved onto the next gentleman in line. A disappointment, to be sure.

It felt like forever before she stood in front of Aaron again. He grinned down at her. "I was wondering, Miss Babineaux, if you would be so kind as to meet me in the library before you retire for the evening. I have something I should like to discuss with you." His voice was low, so as not to carry to the ears of those around them.

Gabby nodded, her pounding heart drowning out the orchestra. "But will you not have to see your guests off after the ball?"

"I had rather hoped you would wait for me."

Oh, she would wait until the sun came up if he asked it of her. Her mind spun with the possibilities, but only one felt the most obvious. Eleanor had said she expected him to offer for Gabby. Did she dare hope that was his intention tonight?

He moved away from her, bowing to the lady now in front of him, but his eyes flicked to hers.

She nodded her head, and his body relaxed. If one was not paying attention, they likely would not have noticed the change. But Gabby did. She noticed everything about him.

The supper dance ended just before midnight. Aaron joined his mother and Rebekah at the fireplace. They each held a branch of greenery in their hands, ceremoniously tossing it into the fire. Gabby looked around. At some point during the evening, the servants had silently removed all the greenery, ensuring bad luck would not haunt Ivydale and her residents for the duration of the new year. She looked up. Regretfully, they had removed all the kissing balls as well.

Aaron offered his arm to Lady Kirtley and led the procession into the great hall for supper.

Mr. Radley held his arm out to Gabby. "Miss Babineaux." He

was not an abhorrent gentleman and would surely be a fine dining partner, just as he had been as a dance partner.

She smiled up at him, but he was no Aaron.

She looked just over Mr. Radley's shoulder, her gaze following Aaron and Eleanor out of the room.

The meal was delicious, or so Gabby heard from those around her. She did not eat much, instead pushing her food around her plate. Her stomach twisted in knots as her mind tried to settle on exactly what it was Aaron wished to speak to her about.

"Do you not agree, Miss Babineaux?"

Gabby paused, staring at her plate. Did she not agree with what?

"I assert if this weather persists, it may keep many people at their country estates, perhaps even starting the Season later than normal."

Gabby shrugged her shoulders before she remembered she was not to do so in social settings. "I am afraid I have no opinion. This is my first Season; I have no previous experience to draw upon." She forked a potato. Perhaps if she put food in her mouth, it would keep others from engaging her in conversation.

She glanced down the table, expecting to see Lady Kirtley's raised brow.

But she was *not* expecting to see Aaron's. One corner of his mouth twitched up.

Gabby blushed. Who else at this table watched him? It seemed obvious to her that he was flirting from afar, but was that just her impression, or did others see it too? Eleanor would surely ring a peal over her head if she took note.

He bit into his roll and licked the butter off his lips.

Gabby tried to pull her eyes away, but they refused to obey her bidding. She knew those lips—knew what they were capable of.

A footman leaned forward and removed her plate, breaking her gaze with Aaron. She blinked several times, feeling eyes on her. The temptation to discover if it was Aaron again was strong, but she didn't know if she could stop herself from staring at him a second time.

Sitting here at the table, she felt very exposed, as if everyone surrounding her could read her every thought and emotion.

Gabby kept her head down as much as possible, smiling and nodding frequently, her focus almost entirely on keeping herself from glancing down to Aaron's side of the table over and over again.

Supper finally ended, and Gabby excused herself. Her face was flushed, and her mind was a flurry of what if's, making it nearly impossible for her to maintain a decent conversation. She needed to find a quiet place and gather herself before Aaron's guests thought her completely daft.

She pushed into the retiring room, nearly collapsing on the settee.

"Good evening, Gabby. Are you having an enjoyable time?" Rebekah poured water into a bowl. Dipping the corner of a serviette into the basin, Rebekah dabbed at her face.

"Yes. It is a lovely ball. I only wish the weather was better so I could get some air."

Rebekah nodded, opening her fan as if to emphasize the point. "It is rather stifling in there." She waited by the door. "Are you coming?"

Gabby shook her head. "I'll be along soon. I need a moment of quiet."

Rebekah fanned herself one more time and flicked it shut. She held the fan out to Gabby. "This may provide the air you need."

Gabby waved the offer away. "I will be well but thank you for the offer."

The door had barely closed behind Rebekah when a servant poked her head in the door. "Miss Babineaux? A note came for you, miss."

Gabby's brow creased. "For me? But from who?" Had Peter discovered she was here? Perhaps he was writing to say he and Caroline would join them here at Ivydale. Although, that seemed unlikely, given they were all to be leaving for London in the next few days.

The maid shrugged. "The footman didn't tell me, miss."

Gabby took the folded paper and turned it over in her hands. No wax sealed the folds, only a series of tucks kept the paper in place.

Gabby unfolded the paper, her curiosity heightened.

The tight scrawl was unfamiliar and gave her no hint as to the sender. Gabby's eyes immediately went to the signature at the bottom. Mrs. Perkins? Why would Mrs. Perkins be sending her a letter?

Gabby started at the top, squinting as she tried to make out the cramped words.

Dear Mademoiselle,

I apologize for any trouble this may cause you, but I need your help. I fear the babe is coming soon, possibly even tonight, and because of my husband's shortsightedness, I now have no blankets to wrap it in. While I know my husband treated you poorly, I pray you will take pity on us and allow us to have the one you offered as a gift. My husband has gone away on business and will not be back til morning. I had hoped to get the blanket this evening and perhaps the herbs you spoke of? I'll send someone to fetch it so as not to inconvenience you any more than I already have. Meet them outside the south door at two.

Yours,

Mrs. Nathan Perkins

Gabby stared at the letter, turning it over in her hand to look at the back as if it would provide some much-needed information. She would give the woman the blanket. That was not a question. But why did she need it tonight? And at such a ridiculous hour? It was normal for parties and balls to run well into the early morning hours, but it wasn't exactly normal to be sending notes to neighbors after midnight. What was more, who would she be sending for the blanket if her husband was away? Not that Gabby had any desire to meet with Mr. Perkins himself.

She looked down at the letter again. There were many misspelled words, and the sentence structure was not precise in all cases. But that was to be expected, was it not? That the woman knew how to write at all impressed Gabby.

She bounced the paper on her opposite hand several times. The entire thing was odd. Something did not feel right, but she could not say exactly what it was. Was it just the timing? Or was there something else?

Gabby sucked her bottom lip into her teeth. She had never given birth, so how was she to know what went through a woman's mind as she neared that time? And a blanket seemed a necessity, especially in weather such as this. If the babe came tonight, could it freeze before morning if they had nothing to wrap it in?

Maybe that was what bothered her. They did not have a single blanket? Or did they not have one suitable for a newborn babe?

She had offered the woman a blanket and some herbs. Perhaps now that her husband was away, she was having second thoughts about rejecting the gift. Gabby dashed her hands upon the cushion at her side. Why was she over analyzing this? A woman had asked for her help. Something that required very little effort on Gabby's part, and here she sat trying to determine the reasons for it.

She pushed herself off the couch and made her way to her room to fetch the blanket and the small satchel of herbs. It was nearly nearing two o'clock, and she did not wish to keep whoever was coming for the package waiting.

Gabby returned downstairs, stopping in the darkened corridor by the south doors. Music drifted faintly from the ballroom on the other side of the house. She leaned her head against the wall. Would Aaron ask for another dance before the night was over?

She looked out into the darkness. Stars sparkled in the sky, as did the moon lighting the night more than she had seen in weeks. The skies were clear of clouds.

Gabby shivered.

It would be a cold night. She was grateful not to be the one coming for this blanket.

The clock in the nearby drawing room chimed two. She stood and looked out the window into the darkness. No one was there, yet.

She turned to sit back down when a shadow from the moonlight moved by the tall bush at the side of the door.

Gabby leaned forward, peering into the darkness. Was that who she was to meet? Why did they not come to the door?

She looked down the corridor. Perhaps they were afraid to be seen this close to the house. She pushed open the doors, immediately chilled to the bone, and stepped outside. Moving toward the bush, she peered around it. "Hello? Is someone there? I have the blanket for Mrs. Perkins."

Snow crunched behind her and Gabby turned, just as rough fabric dropped over her head, casting her in darkness and scratching her cheek and neck. The package dropped from her hands.

Gabby let out a scream, but the burlap covering her head filled her mouth as something closed over her lips, tightening until she could not fully close her mouth. Dust and dirt shook from the fibers, coating her tongue and teeth. She gagged. What was happening?

A vise-like grip tightened around her body and pulled her a short distance. Roughly yanking her gloves from her arms, a rope wrapped tightly around her wrists, binding them behind her. Warmth seeped through the bag with every breath the person took, but it was not in the least comforting.

Her feet left the ground, and her captor threw her over his shoulder. The sounds of the ball faded while the thump and crunch of his footsteps grew louder.

Gabby shivered. Fear and cold battled for prominence, her brain unable to focus on only one of them. Her teeth chattered, and she whimpered. She pushed at the burlap with her tongue, trying to get it out of her mouth, but the bag stayed firmly in place. She tried to speak, to cry out, but no discernable words sounded.

He—she was certain it was Mr. Perkins because of the thumping when he walked—grunted and dropped her onto a cold, wooden floor. It seemed Mr. Perkins was not away from home as the note had indicated.

She moved to sit up, but someone pushed her back down, smacking her face hard into the rough planks beneath her.

"Ye sure about this, Perkins? She didn't look like a spy when I saw her on St. Stephen's Day. I'm worried the major will not be happy about this."

Gabby did not recognize the voice, but whomever it was clearly knew she was the one hidden under the burlap.

"Do not use my name." Perkins growled. "They never look like a spy. That is why she is so dangerous." Mr. Perkins grunted. "The major won't be angry once he's thought about it. I should have thought he would have learned his lesson the last time we encountered Mireille."

They believed her a spy?

She let out a sob and rolled to her side, pulling her legs up to her chest as tightly as she could—both to help her stay warm and out of a sense of preservation.

The floor rocked back and forth before settling into a steady pace. She sucked in a stuttering breath. She was not in a room, but a wagon.

It was taking her from Ivydale. But to where?

There was little sound, save the thundering of her pulse in her ears.

Gabby pulled her legs up tighter. How long would it take Aaron or Eleanor to discover her absence? Would they wait until the ball was over? She shivered, her huddled form no match for the frigid temperatures. She closed her eyes and prayed. If ever there was a time she needed God, it was now.

They had not gone far when the wagon stopped. Someone grabbed Gabby by the ankle and yanked her from the wagon.

She kicked and thrashed, hoping to inflict injury on the men. But without her sight, she did not know if her kicks had landed. Fingernails dug sharply into the soft flesh under her arms; she cried out. All the fight fled, leaving only fear in its place.

The men jerked her upright, placing her feet on the ground. A shove at her back sent her feet stumbling forward, but strong hands gripped her arm tightly, keeping her from sprawling on the ground.

It reminded her of London and the Frost Fair when she had run headlong into Aaron. He had gripped her arms to keep her from falling as well. But there was no gentleness this time. How had she thought him such a brute back then? Even when he disliked her, he'd still been gentle when touching her.

She mumbled, trying to plead with Mr. Perkins or whoever else was with him.

"Keep quiet. We know who you are, Mireille, and we know what you are trying to do." A voice hissed in her ear.

Mireille? Why had he called her that name? He knew what her name was. Gabby had heard him use it before, hadn't she?

They gripped her by the arms tighter, practically dragging her along. Her thin slippers did little to protect her freezing toes from every puddle and bump until her feet scraped against wood.

The smell of hay filled her nostrils. It was warmer in here, but not by much. A hand on her back—so very different from the hand that had guided her around the ballroom earlier—shoved her hard, sending her tumbling to the floor. She braced herself for impact with the hard, wooden floor, but a soft pile of hay caught her instead.

It would have been almost enjoyable, if not for the burning sensation running up her arms and the tingling in her hands. The rope dug deep into her flesh, rubbing away the soft skin.

"You can wait here until dawn, *mademoiselle.*"

What was to happen at dawn? That could not be far off. What if Aaron had not even discovered her missing by then? She mumbled into the burlap and squirmed. Tears of frustration seeped from her eyes.

It was bad enough she was tied up and blindfolded, but to not even be able to talk was almost more than she could bear. How was she to get her answers if she could not even ask the questions?

A deep laugh rumbled and echoed in her ears. "Dawn seems the best time to execute a spy."

Fear gurgled up in Gabby's throat. She bit down on the back of her cheek to keep a fit of hysterics at bay. The metallic taste of blood mixed with dirt filled her mouth. She closed her eyes, drawing her knees up to her chest, and huddled down in the hay. How had she gone from hoping for a second dance with Aaron, to hoping she would live through the night? Maybe if she was lucky, when she opened her eyes, she would discover it had all just been a bad dream.

She took a calming, albeit dusty, breath. Had not Rebekah said Henry had taken all their weapons? What did they mean to execute her with if they had no weapons? Perhaps this charade was meant only to scare her, but not do her any harm. Gabby swallowed, holding on to that thought with all the energy she had left.

CHAPTER 19

Aaron rubbed at his cheeks, trying to remove the ache that came with forcing a smile for the whole of the evening. The only thing keeping him from retiring for the evening was knowing he was to meet Gabby in the library. He wondered if she was there, even now, waiting for him.

He grinned. When he had dressed for this evening, he had no intention of asking for her hand tonight, but after kissing her so thoroughly under the kissing ball, he could think of nothing else. What would it be like to kiss her whenever he desired it?

"Hold on there," he mumbled to himself, pulling on the front of his waistcoat. She had not accepted his offer. Before the kiss, he might have wondered at what her answer would be, but after—he felt quite confident she would accept him.

He shook his head. He would never have believed it possible when she showed up at his home nearly a fortnight ago, that she would be the woman he wished to spend the rest of his life with. Love worked in mysterious ways.

Someone clapped him on the shoulder, and he turned to see Lord and Lady Kirtley at his side.

"Thank you for your generous hospitality, my lord. It was a lovely ball." Lady Kirtley smiled up at him. "I am sure Miss Babineaux had a wonderful time as well." She looked around the empty entryway, her brow creased. "She must not have been feeling well and retired early." The lady glanced over to Rebekah. "Did she speak with you before she left, Lady Brinton?"

Rebekah shook her head. "No, she said she needed some air, but she did not return. She looked rather piqued, so I assumed the same as you—that she retired early."

Aaron tried not to look smug. He should tell them where she was, so they would not worry. But he had already seen Lady Kirtley's reaction to the kissing ball. She would surely not agree to him meeting Gabby alone in the library. Even if it was to ask for Gabby's hand.

"Yes, I would guess it was just a small headache. Nothing a good rest won't remedy." Rest and another sound kiss. That would set Gabby up right. A quiet hum pushed from his lips. He was nearly bursting, yet no one seemed to notice.

"I should bid you all good night. I dare say we are all in need of some sleep." He dipped his head to both Kirtley and his wife, before turning and heading up the stairs. He turned at the top of the first floor toward his study. If someone questioned him, he could make the excuse that he needed to look over some papers before bed. Then he could slip into the library and see Gabby, with Lady Kirtley none the wiser.

He pushed into his study without a word and sat in the chair behind his desk. How long, exactly, did one wait before attending a clandestine meeting? How long would it take until all his house guests were back in their chambers? He beat his thumb on the desktop.

His mother, too taxed to return to the dower house, had retired before the last of the guests had departed. Rebekah had no reason to linger any longer. It had been a long night for everyone. Surely she was halfway to sleep by now.

He ran his hands up and down his thighs, a nervous energy

making his leg jump. The exhaustion he had felt as he bid the last person goodbye had fled. Martin was certainly, even now, wondering where Aaron was. Perhaps he should go to his rooms and release his valet to bed and then go to the library. But even as he thought it, Aaron discarded it.

Gabby had likely been waiting for half of an hour or more. There was no need to keep her waiting any longer.

Aaron moved to the door and pressed his ear to it, listening for any sounds. He felt rather like a spy in his own house, sneaking about and meeting secretly. Gabby would surely find the humor in it.

The house was still. He opened the door a crack and peeked out before stepping into the corridor. He straightened, tugging at his waistcoat. What was he doing, skulking about his own house? He owed no one an explanation, except, perhaps, Gabby.

Taking long strides, no longer caring if someone heard him, Aaron walked to the library and pushed the door open. His mouth turned up in a smile at the anticipation of seeing Gabby.

His eyes went immediately to the settee positioned next to the fireplace; the fire burned low in the grate. But Gabby was not there. He shrugged and scanned the room. When he did not see her below, he knew she must be above, perhaps choosing a new book to read. "Gabby, are you upstairs? I half expected you to be asleep on the couch after waiting so long for me to come." He moved to the middle of the room, where he could see the upper floor, but it, too, was empty.

She was not here? Had she tired of waiting and gone to bed? His brow furrowed. He had asked her to wait for him. Why would she have agreed and then not waited?

The clock on the mantel chimed five times. Aaron dropped his head into his palm. It was five in the morning? It was no wonder Gabby had given up on him and gone to bed. Especially if she had been suffering with a headache. How could he have been so thoughtless as to even ask her to wait up?

His shoulders slumped. He supposed he could wait until

tomorrow to speak with her. After all, what were a few more hours when they would have the rest of their lives together?

He ran a hand through his hair, his earlier fatigue setting in. He was exhausted. Perhaps it was best this way. He would be much more eloquent and convincing—although he hoped she would need little of that—after a good night's sleep.

Striding to the other side of the room, he trudged up the narrow circular steps. Stepping onto the upper level, he gave one last look, just to make sure she was not asleep in any of the chairs up here, before pushing through the door and heading to his own bedchamber.

Martin was dozing in a chair by the fireplace, his elbow resting on the arm and his chin sitting on his palm.

Aaron quietly closed the door behind him, but the click of the lock brought his valet bolt upright. "My lord." His voice was groggy, and he squinted even though the light was low. "Did you have a pleasant evening, sir?"

"Yes. I did. Although, it did not end as I expected." He grunted as Martin pulled off his tailcoat and lay it aside. "But I intend to remedy that tomorrow."

"Anything I can do to help, sir?"

Aaron removed his waistcoat and handed it to the man and then set to work on his cravat. The hazard of having a finely tied knot was that it usually took a great deal of effort to untie it. Aaron shook his head. "No. It is nothing I cannot handle myself."

A quiet knock sounded at the door. Aaron's brow creased. Who would bother him at this time of night? His mind flashed to Gabby. Maybe she had fallen asleep in her room while she waited and had only now awakened. He grabbed his waistcoat and buttoned it over his partially untied cravat, as he hurried over to the door, eager to see her.

Pulling the door open, Aaron took a step back. A small servant he did not recognize stood at his door. "I am sorry to bother you, my lord. But it is Miss Babineaux. She has not returned from zee ball. I have searched zee library and all the rooms I sought she may visit. But she is not zere." This was Gabby's abigail.

What did she mean Gabby had not returned from the ball? He shook his head. "No. You must be mistaken. I was told she left early to get some air and then returned to her room with a headache." Aaron rubbed at his temples with two fingers. No, that was not true. It was all an assumption. But if she had not gone to her room, where was she?

Aaron stepped out into the corridor. "Where have you not looked?"

The maid shook her head. "I have looked everywhere I can sink of."

Collins stepped up onto the landing and cleared his throat. Aaron glanced over at him. Was the entire house awake? "Yes, Collins? What is it?"

"A Mrs. Perkins is at the kitchen door. She insists she needs to speak with you."

Aaron frowned. Mrs. Perkins? What could she want? "Collins, have you seen Miss Babineaux since supper?"

The butler shook his head. "I have not, my lord." He clasped his hands behind his back. "What shall I do about Mrs. Perkins?"

Aaron sighed. He did not have time for her right now. "Tell her to come back in the morning."

Collins cleared his throat. "She says it cannot wait, sir. And judging by the time, I am inclined to believe her."

Aaron shrugged. It was freezing and very early in the morning for a social call. Perhaps Perkins was ill. "Very well, show her to my study please, Collins. And then please come and help Miss Babineaux's maid search the house. She must be here somewhere. If need be, wake up the staff and have them search, as well."

The maid shook her head. "No, please do not go to so much trouble. I am certain I have just not thought of the one place she fell asleep."

Collins nodded. "I will meet you in the west parlor, Aline." He then turned and moved toward the back staircase.

Aaron stepped back into his chambers and grabbed his tailcoat. Sliding it on, he buttoned it as he hopped down the stairs two at a time. He pushed the door to his study open and moved to stir the fire, adding several logs to the grate. The small flames smoked for a moment before flaming to life and slowly licking up the sides of the logs.

A knock sounded and Collins entered with Mrs. Perkins close behind.

The woman looked exhausted, her swollen belly seeming to pull her forward. Dark circles shadowed under large eyes. She looked years older than she had just the other day when he had seen her on St. Stephen's Day.

"Mrs. Perkins, what brings you out on this cold night—" He glanced at the clock. "Or shall I say morning?"

She clutched a handkerchief in her hand, twisting it tightly, then letting it go slack again. "I'm sorry to bother you, my lord. But I fear my husband has made a rash decision."

What was she talking about and why could this not wait until morning? He needed to be looking for Gabby. He ran a hand over his face. "And how can I help?"

She swallowed. "Ever since he returned from the war, he has been different. He is still a good man, my lord, but there are things that vex him real good."

Aaron scrubbed at the back of his neck. He was very aware of what Mr. Perkins's problems were, but they were problems that could wait.

"The French girl you have staying with you, she has him all on edge."

Aaron dropped his hands to his desk and leaned forward. What did Gabby have to do with Perkins's issues? He shook his head, but a thought took hold and a cold chill ran up his back.

"I believe he may have done something to her. He's been

muttering about a Frog spy for days and then went to visit Mr. Millard this evening and he never came home."

Aaron stood quickly, his chair clattering to the floor behind him. "What do you think he has done, Mrs. Perkins?"

Her lip quivered and she shook her head. "I don't know, my lord. I just know he isn't thinking straight."

"Please, go home. You look like you could use the rest. I will find your husband."

A sob wracked her body. "Please, don't hurt him, my lord. He isn't a bad man. He just gets confused sometimes."

Aaron clenched his fists. If Perkins had done something to Gabby, Aaron was not sure he could control himself. He took in a calming breath. "I will do my best."

She nodded and stood up.

Aaron escorted her to the entry. "Wait here. I will have the sledge hitched to take you back to your cottage."

"No need, my lord. I can walk."

Aaron held out a hand, his eye flicking to her belly. "Please, wait."

He headed toward the nearest room and pulled on the cord in the corner. It would likely wake the entire staff, but it was nearing five in the morning. They would all be up soon enough, anyway. And he needed the extra bodies to help look for Gabby, now.

He paced the perimeter of the entry, terrible images of Gabby and where she may be flashing in his mind. What was he going to do? What if they could not find her before his men did something they would all regret?

CHAPTER 20

Even covered in hay, Gabby could not stop her body from shaking. The cold, combined with the fear of what morning would bring, shook her body fiercely.

Her eyes burned when she opened them, both from a lack of sleep and from the dirt that dropped from her lashes every time she blinked.

It felt as if she had been here for days, though she knew it had likely only been hours. She was still alive, after all. The clanking of metal had been her constant companion since her arrival in the dusty, frigid barn. How did they have weapons? While she had never actually heard someone cleaning a gun, she had convinced herself that is what Mr. Perkins and his friend were doing. Readying themselves for their morning task.

It was almost certain Aaron would hear the shot—she guessed that is how they planned to *execute* her—but she could not imagine it would draw him out to investigate. Not unless he had realized she was gone. Had Aline told him?

Aaron. Her chest constricted and her throat tightened painfully. She would never see him again. It seemed almost cruel that they had overcome their dislike of each other—possibly come to love each other —only to have it end like this. She would never dance with him at Almack's or attend the theatre. There would be no walks along the Serpentine in Hyde Park or even around the gardens here at Ivydale.

Her breath hitched as another bout of tears threatened. She had been pushing them off since the dratted bag had been thrown over her head.

She turned her thoughts back to Aaron. As sad as it made her to know their time was over, thinking on him still brought a measure of peace and joy to her heart. Would he think of her when he went into the library? She hoped so—though she hoped they would be happy thoughts.

A knock sounded on wood somewhere close by and Gabby straightened, turning an ear toward the sound.

"Who's there?" Mr. Perkins's gruff voice asked and he thump-stepped away from her.

"It's Major Campbell, Perkins. I need to speak to you."

Gabby squeaked. It was Aaron. He had found her.

"He knows, Nathan," the other man whispered fiercely. "We're going to be sent to Newgate, for sure."

"Keep your mouth shut, Millard." There was a small scuffle before Mr. Perkins answered. "It's a bit early, Major, sir. Perhaps you can come back later?"

Even Gabby could hear the guilt in the man's voice.

"No. Open the door, Ensign. I have not yet sent for the Constable, but I will if I must."

Gabby heard the scratching of wood. Was Mr. Perkins opening the door?

The shakes wracking her body intensified with the anticipation not just of being saved, but of seeing Aaron again.

The door groaned as it opened, and footsteps sounded.

"Where is she?" Never had she welcomed the gravelly tone as she did now, even if it was near frantic. It was closer now, but still, Gabby could tell Aaron was on the other side of the barn.

She squirmed and squeaked, trying to get him to come in her direction.

"Who, Major?"

"You know who I mean. Miss Babineaux. What have you done with her?" His voice got louder, but she did not know if it was because he drew closer or had simply started yelling.

"I don't rightly know, sir." Perkins sounded as though he were moving quickly, his foot and peg scratching on the ground as if he were trying to keep in front of Aaron. "We only wanted to scare her back to France, sir."

Gabby screamed as loud as she could—which was weak at best due to the gag in her mouth—but she did not know if it could be heard over the nickering horses.

"Thunder and turf, man." Aaron was close; she could almost feel his warmth. "What have you done?" Gentle hands lifted her from the hay. "Gabby?"

"Major, you are making a mistake...again. She is a spy."

"Kirtley. Please help Paul and Marcus escort these two men to the house. I will deal with them once Gabby is safe."

"Are you certain you don't need me here?" It was only now Gabby heard Lord Kirtley's voice. Who else was there with them?

One of Aaron's hands dropped from her arm but was quickly replaced again. "Yes. I would prefer you aid in securing the men who did this to her."

"But there will be no one here with you. Eleanor..." Kirtley trailed off. "Very well. I will meet you back at the house."

"I am going to untie the cloth from your mouth. Hold still." Aaron's breath shook as her head jerked to one side and then the other with each tug he gave on the band.

It fell away, and Gabby closed her mouth, working her jaw without taking in more dust and dirt.

The bag came off and Gabby squinted.

Aaron's shining eyes and creased brow peered down at her. There were many times she had thought him more handsome than anyone of her acquaintance, but those times paled compared to now. Never had she been so happy to see anyone, but especially him. And from the way he looked down at her now, she had no doubt he loved her.

"Aaron." Her voice rasped.

He shifted on his knees, and she could tell he was biting his cheek. He lifted a shaking hand to her face and using his thumb, wiped away the dirt under her eye. "Look at you."

"I must look a fright."

He shook his head. "You are the loveliest sight I've ever seen."

"I thought the same of you." After keeping them in for hours, tears spilled over, wetting his fingers and her cheeks.

"I'm sorry, Gabby." He held her face in both hands. His tenderness making her sob. "How did I not see this would happen?"

She shook her head. "No." Her throat burned from dryness. "The fault is mine. I should never have come to visit Mrs. Perkins. Not after St. Stephen's Day. I knew..." A sob choked out again.

"You went..." He shook his head. "We can discuss that later." He looked down, likely wondering why she had not embraced him, and his eyes widened. Swatting hay out of his way, he moved behind her.

Aaron swore. "Oh, Gabby. I don't think I can untie these without causing you pain."

"It cannot hurt more than it does now. Please, release them."

He worked at the knots and Gabby bit down on her lip. She had been wrong. It hurt much worse. The fibers of the rope clawed at her flesh as if they were reluctant to let her go. But finally, her hands dropped free. She pulled them to her front and dropped them in her lap. Lifting and dropping her shoulders, she worked a few of the kinks out. She dared not touch the skin around her wrists, the soft lace of her gown caused enough of a sting.

Gabby stared down at her gown, now ripped and streaked with blood from her swollen wrists. It had been such a lovely gown—so full of promise.

Aaron kneeled in front of her and sighed. He removed his greatcoat and draped it over her shoulders.

"But what will you wear? You will freeze."

He dropped his forehead to hers. "Let me do the worrying for a time." He slid his arms beneath her knees and one behind her back, lifting her into his arms and cradling her to him. "Come. Let us get you back to Ivydale."

Gabby rested her head against his superfine coat, breathing in the scent of him. "I am certain I can walk."

A shaky chuckle sounded. "Yes, I am sure you are able, but I find I like this remarkably better. It is the only way I can assure myself you are truly safe." As if to emphasize his point, he tightened his hold on her, bringing her firmly into him. "It makes up only slightly for the fact I did not get a second dance with you."

He set her down, only long enough to mount his horse, and then Collins helped lift her onto Aaron's saddle. Again, he pulled her tightly to him. "Put your arms around me, under my coat so they will stay warm."

"But they are bloody. They will ruin your waistcoat."

"I have many waistcoats, Gabby, but only one you. You need to get warm. I can feel the cold on your skin through my coats."

It was strange. She had never felt more wanted and even needed than she did right then. But how could that be? She had been the one in need of rescue.

Aaron touched his heels to his horse's side and clucked, setting the horse into an easy stride. She was grateful he had not set him into a canter, just yet. Her wrists—in truth, her whole body—ached, but she tightened her hold on him even more.

Aaron's heart still pounded inside his chest. He tightened his hold on Gabby, just to assure himself that she was safe and well. Well might be a stretch of the truth. She looked a sight, though a more lovely sight he had never seen.

When he thought about what could have happened...would have happened had he not arrived when he did, tears pricked at his eyes. He recalled the rifles lying next to the bales of hay, cleaned and ready for firing, a shiver straightened his spine.

He dug his heels into Bruce's side and the horse picked up speed. It was a tricky business getting them home quickly, but without causing Gabby any more pain. Bruce seemed to understand and stepped lightly, delivering them to Ivydale with little wincing from Gabby.

Aaron swung down from the saddle and reached up, pulling Gabby back into his arms. He did not feel completely at ease unless she was in his arms. But he doubted she would agree to staying here indefinitely.

"You should put me down now," she whispered against his neck.

His pulse ticked up, but this time it wasn't from fear. He sighed. "I am not putting you down, Gabby. Not until we are safely in the house and outside your bedchamber door, where I will hand you off to Aline."

"Don't be daft, Aaron. I am perfectly capable of walking. You are going to give people a false impression of our association."

He heard the measured tone of her words. She was suggesting he would make people think they were engaged, but she did not actually say the words. Aaron looked down, a crooked smile on his face. "I told you to let me do the worrying for now."

"But Eleanor—"

He didn't have to reach for the knob as Marcus was waiting for them and swung it open as soon as Aaron's feet had planted on the landing. "I do not care about Eleanor." His voice echoed as he stepped into the entryway.

A sharp intake of breath, followed by a hearty laugh followed, but Aaron only half-heartedly regretted his words. He *did not* care about Eleanor. The only woman he cared a wit about, was in his arms, pressed against his chest.

"Lud," he muttered as he eyed Kirtley and his wife. Why was no one asleep or somewhere other than here? Did they not understand he wanted Gabby to himself?

He growled as Gabby wiggled away from him, forcing him to lower her to the ground. He removed his greatcoat from her shoulders and handed it to Collins. Leaning in, he whispered, "Did I not say I would carry you until I deposited you at your bedroom door?"

Her ears pinked, but she did not reply.

Lord and Lady Kirtley hurried the rest of the way down the stairs, and Lady Kirtley enveloped Gabby in a hug. "Oh, Gabby. I was so worried about you." The lady reached for Gabby's hands, but Gabby pulled back, leaning into Aaron.

Lady Kirtley looked hurt.

Gabby lifted her wrists. Lady Kirtley gasped, again. "Oh, dearest. Come, let us get you warmed up and bandage those cuts. I have already called for a tub and hot water." She put her hand on Gabby's back and moved her toward the stairs. Casting a glance at Kirtley and Aaron, she lowered her voice. "I expect you will see to the men who did this to her."

Aaron growled. This was precisely why he did not want others about. Lady Kirtley was doing what Aaron had wanted to do. She was taking over the care of Gabby.

A pain burned in Aaron's chest. While he knew Gabby was safe now, fear that something may happen to her still, caused his heart to hammer. "Wait," he called. Must she be out of his sight—away from his protection?

Gabby turned at the same time as Lady Kirtley.

He stepped forward, placing a gentle hand on her face. "There are things we need to discuss. I'm afraid it cannot wait." It could wait, and he felt a sliver of guilt when he looked into her tired eyes. He should let her go to bed, but he could not. Not yet. He had waited for the right time to ask her before, and he had nearly lost his chance—nearly lost her. He glanced at Kirtley. "Are the men in my study?"

Gabby stiffened. She was genuinely afraid of Mr. Perkins and Mr. Millard. And she had good reason to be.

Aaron fisted his hands at his side. If they were all still in the army...but they were not. He would contact the constable and see them sent to Newgate, at the very least.

Kirtley nodded. "Marcus is standing guard, should they try to escape."

Aaron looked to Lady Kirtley. "I will return her shortly." Although, he did not know if he could actually turn her over to Lady Kirtley when he was done with her. If they were engaged, as he planned to take care of immediately, would he be allowed to watch her sleep? If only he had a special license hanging about his study...

He shook his head. He sounded on the verge of Bedlam, but he could hardly help it. Whenever his eyes shut for any extended amount of time, the picture of her bound with the burlap sack on her head flashed through his mind, and his heart set to racing all over again.

He moved his hand from her face to the small of her back. "Come. I will not keep you from Eleanor's fussing for long." He led her up the stairs and down the corridor. She walked stiffly, her muscles taut. She was likely feeling the aftereffects of her ordeal.

He stopped at the library door. "Let us talk in here."

The air whooshed from her lungs, and she sagged against the wall.

Aaron's heart stopped. "Gabby, what is wrong?" His body went cold. Was she suffering from something he could not see? He reached for her, sliding his hand around her waist to support her. "Let me help you to a couch inside."

She melted against him, but then pushed him away. "No, I am well. I can walk unassisted."

"But in the corridor, you looked as if you might faint." He held his hand at the ready in front of him in case she fell again.

Gabby shook her head. "I thought you were to take me to your study, to speak with those men. I am simply relieved that you brought me here, instead."

She thought he would make her see those two blackguards? Did she not know him better? "How could you think I would allow you to see them again?"

"I'm sorry. I..." She paused. "What did you wish to discuss with me?"

He paused. He had meant to ask for her hand first, but her fear reminded him he needed to deal with those men now and get them out of his house—off of his property.

He lightly gripped her by the upper arms. "I cannot do this, Gabby. I am being a selfish cad." He sagged. She looked as if she may fall asleep while standing here listening to him. "You look so cold and tired. What I wish to say can wait until you are rested and warm." As much as he wanted to ask her to wait in here for him, he could not do it. "Please, come find me here when you awaken. I wish to speak to you as soon as possible."

"Do you wish me to wait?"

Yes, I want you to never leave my sight. "No. You need to get warm and get some rest." He ran his thumb over her cheekbone. "I will wait for you this time."

She turned toward the door but paused. "Aaron?"

"Yes?" Was she going to stay after all?

"Please, do not punish them."

He lurched forward. The mention of the men waiting in his office left him needing her close. "What? I most certainly will punish them. They were intent on killing you, Gabby."

She turned around. "They were not in their right minds. Mr. Perkins called me Mireille." She bit her bottom lip. Ah, that look. He did not think he could deny her anything when she gave him that look. She would quickly come to realize the power she held over him.

"That is no excuse. What about the next time he is not in his right mind?"

She twisted her hands together. "I will be...leaving soon." She paused as if giving him the opportunity to refute her. But he did not. He did not like what she was saying and was not about to change the subject.

"I cannot look on them without remembering what they have done. They cannot stay here."

She frowned. "Could you move them to a different estate? They only have negative experiences with Mireille. What if we could give them another experience? A good one? Perhaps it would change the way they think."

This woman was...astounding. Aaron could not feel even an ounce of forgiveness toward the men. If it were up to him, they would be at Newgate before the rising of the sun. But he would do as she wanted. "Is this what you truly want?"

She nodded. "Yes, it is."

"Then I will see to it." He could not do otherwise.

"Thank you." She turned and slipped from the room.

He felt her absence immediately, and his hands became wet and shaky. Would he ever feel she was safe when they were not together? His anger increased at this new aspect of his life. Although, as he thought on it, it also brought on a sense of wonder. He had always had men to worry about. But never had he worried about a woman, not like this, anyway.

He growled and pounded his fist into his hand. Now would be a good time to see his *men*. He could hardly stomach calling them that any longer.

CHAPTER 21

"I will see to the prisoners now, Marcus." Aaron paused outside his study door, clutching his fists at his sides. If Gabby could forgive them, then he should too. But it was easier said than done.

He breathed deeply and pushed into the room.

His nostrils flared when the men turned in their seats to watch his approach. Both men held their hat in their hands, rotating them round and round. "Major—"

"It is *Lord* Brinton now." His voice was terse and clipped.

"Begging your pardon, my lord." Mr. Millard's eyes dropped to his hands.

Aaron moved behind his desk. Dropping his hands on the table, he leaned forward and sucked in a deep breath. *Gabby forgives them.* He repeated it over and over in his mind, hoping it would help him do the same. "What the devil did you think you were doing?" Perhaps he would need to say it a few more times for it to fully take hold.

"I see my mistake now, my lord. But...she sounded so much like—and she kept coming around, trying to get my wife to betray me—to betray us." Perkins shook his head and looked down at his hat. His brow furrowed and his lips moved but no sound came out.

Both men looked contrite, but Aaron had difficulty accepting it. What if he had not found her in time? What if Mrs. Perkins had not come to see him? There were so many terrible outcomes from this situation. How could he just let these men go?

"I understand I am bound for Newgate, in the best case, but I beg for my wife. Please allow her to stay, at least until the babe is born." Tears hovered in the bottoms of Perkins's lids.

Aaron felt himself softening slightly. It had not been so long ago that he saw Mireille when he looked on Gabby? Lud, that felt like eons ago. Aaron had changed. But would these men really learn anything if they were not punished?

From Henry's letters, Aaron knew Rebekah cared for Mrs. Perkins; perhaps it was possible Aaron could send the couple and Millard to Charlcombe. Although, after hearing what Mr. Perkins had done, would Rebekah agree to it? Neither of the men had ever been threatening to her, so it was a possibility. They could help ready the house and once the weather warmed, begin work on their farms there. But was relocation punishment enough?

Aaron sat down and leaned back in his chair, crossing his arms across his chest. "I have spoken with Miss Babineaux and have agreed to abide by her wishes in this matter."

Both men ducked their heads, their hands spinning the hats faster.

"She has asked for you to return to your farms until such time as the weather lifts and you can relocate to a different property. I will send out inquiries immediately to find where that will be, precisely. Until that time, you are not to come near the house. Is that understood?" He would not mention Charlcombe until he had confirmed it with Rebekah.

Mr. Perkins's mouth dropped open. "You aren't sending us to Newgate?"

Aaron shook his head. "You will find Miss Babineaux is nothing like Mireille. She is kind, even to those so undeserving of it. You do not deserve her grace, but she is offering it all the same." He narrowed his eyes at them. "I would not be so forgiving. I suggest you consider this act in the future, for if I hear of any other incidents—"

"There will be no other incidents, my lord. You have my word." Mr. Millard stood, obviously wishing to leave before Aaron changed his mind.

Aaron stood. "Very well. Mr. Perkins, please go attend to your wife. I fear the anxiety of last night's activities were not beneficial to her in her condition."

Perkin's looked even more remorseful. He glanced up. "May I offer Miss Babineaux my thanks?"

Aaron's eyes widened and he opened his mouth, but Perkins cut him off with a shake of his head.

"No, no. You are right, my lord. Perhaps a letter would be best."

Millard grabbed Perkins by the coat and pulled him toward the door, bowing several times. "Many thanks, my lord. And good day." They got to the door and fled quickly from the room.

Aaron raised his brows. He never knew Perkins peg leg could move so quickly. But they had the right of it.

He rubbed at his burning eyes. The anxiety and stress of the night finally faded, leaving him exhausted. Perhaps it would be best if he rested before he spoke to Gabby.

Gabby ran her hands down the front of her morning gown and stared at the wooden door. What would she find on the other side? Aaron had told her to find him in the library when she woke, but that had been hours ago. Surely, he was not still waiting for her. He had certainly been as tired as she had been.

She opened the door and peered in, disappointed when he did not appear to be inside. Should she wait for him? She had told him she would wait last night after the ball, but that had not gone according to plan. Why could she not wait for him now?

She slipped inside, shutting the door behind her. She would sit on the couch and wait until he came.

She scanned the shelves as she passed. A book would certainly make the time go faster, but she was not in the mood to read. She was too jumpy to sit still and focus on words. Wrapping her arms around her middle, she walked toward a chair by the fire. Today she was in the mood to sit and do nothing. Even if it meant thinking back on the awful events of last night.

In the light of day, she could think on them with only a tendril of fear. The more she thought on what she'd endured, the easier it would become, would it not?

As she moved to the sofa, she stopped, her head dropping to the side and a smile filling her face.

Aaron lay on the couch, his head resting on an embroidered cushion. His breath was slow and low. His hair stuck up in all directions, lifting off his forehead. The light from the fire reflected the hints of gold in his hair.

His superfine tailcoat was unbuttoned, exposing a light blue waistcoat. It was the same clothes he had worn to the ball last night. She noted, with appreciation, the slight stubble darkening his cheeks and chin. It did not appear he had returned to his chambers yet. Was it because he had been anxious to see her? The thought made her slightly lightheaded.

She moved quietly and kneeled on the floor beside the sofa. Lifting her hand toward his face, she ran her fingertips over the stubble on his cheek and up into the hair over his ear. It was softer than she had even imagined.

Gooseflesh prickled her skin as she realized what she was doing.

He breathed in deeply and she pulled her hand away, biting her lip. Had she awakened him?

"Please, do not stop or I shall believe I am only dreaming."

She sat back on her heels. "I'm sorry. I did not intend to wake you."

His eyes remained closed. "I was not asleep. It was all a part of my plan." He cracked a single eye open.

She looked at him blandly. "Oh? Am I so predictable that you knew if you pretended to be asleep, I would caress your cheek?" Saying it out loud sounded so intimate and improper. Her cheeks warmed.

He opened both his eyes and bounced his brows. "Indeed. I knew you would not be able to resist." Then he winked—the flirt.

"You know me too well, my lord." She stared at him. Eleanor had told her the weather had improved enough that they would be setting out for London the next morning. How was she to leave this man? Her heart would surely break. What if things changed when they went to London?

The last few days, with the exception of the kidnapping, Gabby had felt as if she was living in a bubble that could burst at any moment and change everything. If she stayed here at Ivydale indefinitely, could she stay in the bubble forever?

"I thought I asked you not to stop what you were doing."

She smirked. "It is not so proper now that I know you are awake."

He pinched his eyes closed. "Is this better?"

"Your talking is ruining the illusion of you being asleep, Aaron." She chuckled but raised her hand to his cheek once more. Her knuckles brushed lightly down his cheek bone and along his jaw to the other side of his face. When she stilled for a moment, Aaron placed his hand over hers and turned his head, kissing the palm of her hand.

Her breath hitched and she hoped the bubble never broke. "Now that you have awakened, did you not wish to talk?" Her voice came out wobbly. "You said it was important."

He growled. "It could certainly wait a few minutes longer." He swung his legs to the floor and sat up. "I was rather enjoying your diversion."

She raised a brow at him. "You are the one who said it was important that we speak immediately. And as we will be leaving on the morrow..." She sighed. Would he be as disappointed as she was?

"Yes, I did say such things." He paused mid-shrug. "Did you say you are leaving tomorrow?"

Gabby nodded. "Yes. We are returning to London."

He pushed himself to standing and reached down for her hands. Tugging her gently to her feet, he pulled her to face him, leaving only inches between them.

Gabby was suddenly nervous. She pulled her hands from his and ran them down the front of her skirt. "Did you settle things with the men?" Why was she bringing them up now? She still could not think their names without her hands shaking. Although, she did not completely believe they were the reason for her jittery hands and legs.

"Yes. They will stay on their farms until the weather lifts. Then my hope is they will accompany Rebekah to Charlcombe. It would be best for all of them." He sighed. "They wished to thank you for your kindness, but I persuaded them to do so in a letter."

Gabby breathed in through her nose. "Thank you. I think that best."

He leaned slightly in and his breath fluttered the curl at her cheek.

Her eyes fluttered shut briefly. She ran her thumb and index finger down a fold at the side of her skirt. "You said there were things we needed to discuss—things that could not wait."

He lifted his hands and she thought for a moment he would cup her cheeks like he had done in the barn. But he rested them on her upper arms, instead and pulled her a step closer to him. His unbuttoned tailcoat grazed against her arms. "Yes. They are very serious things."

She dropped her eyes to the floor. Would he ask her what had happened last night—how she had come to be abducted? He had asked her nothing about it, not even what had happened while she was in the barn. Surely, he was curious.

While it would be easier to discuss now than it had been early this morning, she still felt hesitant. They had very little time left together, and she did not want to waste it by reliving the events of early this morning.

Aaron shifted closer to her and his hands dropped to her forearms. "There are many things I wish to discuss with you. Your favorite books, plays, even your favorite ice at Gunthers. But all those things can wait." Featherlight, his fingertips danced up her arms and gooseflesh raised on her skin.

Aaron grinned. "If you will recall, I had asked you to meet me here after the ball." He let his hand rest at her hips, tugging her to within a whisper of him.

Gabby sucked in a breath. She would never have guessed a fortnight ago the playful nature she was seeing in Aaron now.

His hands slid behind her, and he clasped them together at the small of her back.

For a moment all thought fled from her brain. His gray-blue eyes the only thing she could comprehend.

His fingers rubbed small circles on the small of her back.

It was heavenly and she did not want him to stop. But then Eleanor's shocked face from the doorway of the ballroom pushed its way into her mind. This embrace, as wonderful as it felt—and because of the way it felt—was improper.

She pushed against his chest, putting only a small amount of distance between them because he would not unclasp his fingers.

He stared down at her, a hint of doubt suddenly clouding his eyes. "Gabrielle, I asked you to come here because I wished to ask for your hand."

Why should he want her hands? Her brain felt muddled. Surely it was the smell of lemon, bergamot, and rosemary emanating from him that was clouding her brain. She lifted her hands from his chest so he could see them. "But my hands are all scratched and swollen. Why would you want them?"

"For so very many reasons, *mon amour*. So you may run them along my face and in my hair, just to name one." He chuckled and leaning down, brushed his lips against hers. He pressed against her back until her hands rested again on his chest.

She blinked several times before her eyes fluttered closed and she leaned fully into his kiss. Memories of the kissing ball and those moments in the barn when she worried she would never see him again flooded her mind, and she clung tighter to him.

He pulled back and grinned down at her. "Now that I have your focus where it should be..." He paused.

Her focus? For all the thoughts swirling in her brain, she had a brief moment of clarity. Her mouth formed an O and she nodded. "Oh, you want my *hand*."

He grinned wickedly. "I want all of you, but for this conversation, your hand is all I require." He rested his brow against hers. "When I kissed you under the kissing ball, I knew then that I never wanted anyone else. Only you would do. And then when I thought I had lost you—thought I was too late, I realized how fast everything can change. I don't want to have to wait—even for the banns—to make you mine."

She tipped her head back, a smile hovering on her lips. How could it be that this man wanted her? "Does that mean you have a special license in your pocket, Aaron? If not, I fear you will need to go at least several days before making me your wife."

He grunted. "No. But as you saw on the sofa earlier, I am a planner. I just have not settled on which plan to go with, just yet. I thought perhaps you could help me with that."

She ran her thumb along his bottom lip, and he let out a quiet sort of whimper. It was practically sinful that he should look as he did and have perfect lips as well.

"You are not going to make the next few days easy on me, are you *mon amour*?"

She shivered in his arms at his new name for her. "What are the options, my lord?"

He scowled when she pulled her thumb away. "I either have to wait three weeks for the banns to make you mine—which I have already told you I do not wish to do—or dash to London and arrange for an audience with the Archbishop of Canterbury. Either option does require me to wait." He scowled. "I do not like to wait."

Gabby tapped her lip and his eyes watched every move. "It would seem the second plan is best, as we are to leave for London in the morning."

His eyes twinkled. "Ah, so we are."

She grinned. "We?"

He guffawed. "If you think I am letting you out of my sight, you are quite mad. I will be returning to London tomorrow, as well. I am certain my mother would be more than happy to act as chaperone on our trip back." He gently intertwined his fingers on her back. "But I am being selfish, again. I have only told you what I want." He kissed the tip of her nose. "If you should wish to wait for the banns to be posted, I shall do my best to be patient."

"My only wish is to be with you...always. I confess," her face warmed at what she was about to admit, "when I was playing with your hair earlier, all I could think about was how I could not bear to be away from you when we left tomorrow."

"I know the feeling." He dropped his forehead to hers. "When I didn't know where you were last night, I thought it was the longest hours of my life. But somehow, I think the time between now and when we can be married, will feel far longer than even that." He released her fingers from his but captured her hand and pressed it over his heart. "Because in here, you are already mine forever and always."

EPILOGUE

Gabby sat in a chair along the wall of Lord Huntington's ballroom. This was the first ball of the Season. Thus far, she had not been shunned by the Ton as she had feared. But she had not been all the rage, either. Several men had asked her to dance and there had been a fair amount of sets that she had sat out.

She was not sure if her marriage or her heritage were the cause, but she did not care which was the culprit. She had what she wanted. All of this...she glanced around her at the glittering candlelight and fine gowns before her. All of this was just a façade. An image that was not wholly real.

A hand dropped onto her shoulder and squeezed gently. "How are you enjoying the ball, *mon amour*?"

Gabby shivered under Aaron's touch and at his words. He had called her his love for weeks now, but still it thrilled her to her bones. "It is lovely."

He grasped her hand and pulled her to stand beside him. "That was not an answer to my question."

Gabby shrugged. "I am enjoying myself."

Aaron tilted his head to the side. "But..."

She sighed. "But I should far prefer to be at home with you."

"Then let us be on our way. I shall inform my mother and call for the carriage while you fetch your wrap." He pulled her along, but with such a gentleness she could only smile at his back.

As they stepped into the entryway, she pulled him to a stop and he turned to face her. "It will be intolerably rude to leave early, will it not?"

He shook his head. "Not if you are feeling ill." He placed his gloved hand to her forehead. "My dear, you feel warm. Are you feeling ill?" His voice raised in volume.

"Dreadfully." She grinned at him.

"It is just as I suspected, we must return home." He kept his voice raised for the benefit of those around them but leaned in and whispered in her ear. "*Mon amour*, you might wish to stop smiling, it will give our ruse away." He motioned to a nearby footman and asked for the carriage and Gabby's wrap to be fetched.

Gabby pursed her lips closed and tried to look ill. How did one look ill when they really were not? She placed her fingertips to her temple.

"Nice touch, my dear. If I did not know better, I should think you truly were ill." Aaron placed a quick kiss in her hair. "We will be on our way soon." He continued to play his part.

Eleanor stepped from a nearby hallway. She pushed at her hair and looked around the entryway.

Gabby raised a hand and offered a small wave, just as their gazes connected.

Eleanor changed directions and came to stand beside them. "What is it? Why do you look as if you are waiting for your carriage?"

Gabby swallowed, hating lying to her friend. "I am..."

"She is not feeling well. I am taking her home to rest." It seemed Aaron had no such qualms about lying to Eleanor.

Eleanor's face creased with worry. "You have not caught a cold, have you?"

Gabby shook her head. "I believe it is merely a headache. I will be well after some rest."

Eleanor eyed her and then Aaron, who looked altogether too happy to be leaving. "You are certain you will be well?" She asked again.

Gabby nodded. "Yes, Eleanor. Why do you not come for tea tomorrow and you may see for yourself?"

Eleanor smiled and patted Gabby on the hand. "I should love to join you." She glanced at Aaron and then back to Gabby. "Have a wonderful, quiet time at home."

Gabby grinned and Aaron whispered a reminder. "Looking much too happy."

"Run along now. I am certain your carriage has arrived." Eleanor shifted more toward Aaron. "And do not worry. I shall inform your mother. Hugh and I will bring her home with us."

"Thank you, Eleanor." He took the wrap from the footman standing at his arm and placed it over Gabby's shoulders. He glanced back at Eleanor but spoke to Gabby. "You see, I told you she was not such a grump."

At Eleanor's intake of breath, Aaron chuckled and wrapped his arm around Gabby's waist, supporting her as one might a fake ailing wife. "Come, dearest. Let us get you home." He winked at down her.

"And you think it is my smiles that will ruin our charade?" She tsked as they made their way out the front doors and to their waiting carriage.

Just over an hour later, Aaron stretched out on the couch, his cravat discarded and his tailcoat draped over the back of a chair. The library was quiet. Too quiet. What was taking Gabby so long to join him?

The door opened almost soundlessly. Only the swishing of

Gabby's skirts alerted him to her presence. "I was beginning to think perhaps you were ill and had gone to bed."

"I would have to be very ill, indeed, to stay away from our time in the library." She approached the couch and Aaron sat up.

Gabby reached for the book on the side table and sat down, drawing Aaron's head onto her lap. She opened the book to the marked page and held it in one hand as she began to read in French.

Aaron sighed as her other fingers lightly caressed one cheek and then the other. She moved to his nose and up his brow before splaying her fingers out into his hair. "Ah, why do we even bother to leave the house, when this is so much more enjoyable?"

Gabby's voice wobbled slightly as she smiled. "We cannot stay in every night, my love. People will whisper."

Aaron closed his eyes and pulled her hand from his face. Intertwining their fingers, he rested their hands on his chest. "Let them whisper, *mon amour*. Yours is the only voice I wish to hear."

AFTERWORD

Dear Reader,

Thank you so much for reading! I hope you love this story as much as I do.

When I wrote Unmasking Lady Caroline, I knew that I wanted Gabby to have her own story. She was such a unique character and I loved her. I was excited I was able to find a man that was perfect for her, even if they did not think so in the beginning.

As a note on the setting of the Frost Fair. This was an actual event that took place in late January and early February of 1814. But for the sake of the story I moved the event forward a month. However, the descriptions of the fair are accurate.

You can stay up to date on all of my author happenings by signing up for my newsletter.

Be sure to check out my other stories:

Unlikely Match Series:

An American in Duke's Clothing

The Baron's Rose

A Princess for the Gentleman

Regency House Party Series

Mistaken Identity

Miss Marleigh's Pirate Lord

Scoundrel's Rake and Rogues Series

Reforming the Gambler

Rake on the Run

The Belles of Christmas Series

Unmasking Lady Caroline

Contemporary Romances

Top Flight Series

Bear: A Fighter Pilot Romance

Mustang: A Fighter Pilot Romance

Happy reading!

Mindy

ACKNOWLEDGMENTS

To Jenny Proctor, my fabulous editor who helps me with my comma addiction and gives great insight when I have used all of mine up.

For my great Regency critique peeps: Dickens, Heyer, Bronte and Austen, Esther and Anneka! You guys are amazing and only make me want to be better. I'm grateful to call you my friends!

To my beta readers and proof-readers: Kim Ball and Patti Knowlton, Kendra, Michelle, Camille, Maria, Marilee, and Stacey—many thanks for all your help. I truly could not do this without all of you!

To my great ARC team. Thank you for all you do to help me be successful! You guys are the best!

And last and most importantly, for my boys. You guys are why I do this. Thanks for being patient when you want me to do other things besides write. I couldn't do this without your support! LY

ABOUT THE AUTHOR

Mindy loves all things history and romance, which makes reading and writing romance right up her alley. Since she was a little girl, playing in her closet "elevator," she has always had stories running through her mind as she visited exotic places.

But it wasn't until she was well into adulthood, that she realized she could write those stories down. Now they occupy her dreams and most every quiet moment she has-she often washes her hair two or three times because she wasn't paying attention when she did it the first time. Which usually means really clean hair and a fixed plot hole.

When she isn't living in her alternate realities, she is married to her real-life Mr. Darcy and trying to raise five proper boys. They live happily in the beautiful mountains of Utah.

Stay up to date on any upcoming releases by signing up for her newsletter.

ALSO BY MINDY BURBIDGE STRUNK

Unlikely Match Series:

An American in Duke's Clothing

The Baron's Rose

A Princess for the Gentleman

Regency House Party Series

Mistaken Identity

Miss Marleigh's Pirate Lord

Scoundrel's Rake and Rogues Series

Reforming the Gambler

Rake on the Run

The Belles of Christmas Series

Unmasking Lady Caroline

Contemporary Romances

Top Flight Series

Bear: A Fighter Pilot Romance

Mustang: A Fighter Pilot Romance